# UNTAMED

Alexandra Wright

www.BOROUGHSPUBLISHINGGROUP.com

UNTAMED
Copyright © 2019 Ingrid Mazaleigue

ISBN 978-1-948029-81-0

*For Fiona*

# ACKNOWLEDGMENTS

Thank you to my mum, Judy, who encouraged me to choose my own path in life, and to Vidar for being my confidante, my closest friend, and my most enthusiastic fan. Your unwavering love and support gives me wings. Thank you to dear friends and fellow writers who believed in me. And, lastly, to the Boroughs Publishing Group team for your faith in my books.

# UNTAMED

# Chapter One

At the ripe old age of seventeen, Belle knew that boys were only interested in a certain type of girl: the ones who were well developed, pretty, and willing to compromise themselves for attention. The boys liked girls who were confident, ambitious and flirty. That was the way it was. And Belle suspected that it had little to do with the fact that they were still only boys. You only had to open any magazine to know that those boys became men who were interested in precisely the same thing.

Though the taunts and jibes stung, Belle didn't really mind being alone. It suited her. Crowds of people drained her energy and made her long for solitude. She contented herself with caring for her brother, helping her mother and, of course, her secret hobby of sketching strangers.

If it was an odd pastime, as she suspected it was, she didn't much care. Belle never felt more alive, more herself than when she was drawing. Especially when she was balanced on the broad branches of the Autumn Flame maple that stretched its majestic branches from the center of her family's backyard. It was a good enough life for a girl from a small town who was five foot eleven, awkward and had flame-red hair. She had never dared to hope for more.

Her hand was almost a blur as it skimmed over the page, recreating the lines and planes of the old woman's face. Belle scarcely glanced at the page as she worked, her eyes trained to every detail, every curve, every feature as, she scrutinized the stranger.

A thrill shot through her as she looked down at her work. There it was, yet again. Magically, it seemed, she had captured the essence of the sweet little old lady. A quality that could not be seen with eyes alone. Belle wasn't sure how she did it, but it always gave her a buzz, a little peal of happiness, to know that she had created something that showed a person's true beauty.

The woman happened to look up as Belle was adding the finishing touches to her sketch. She felt a jolt of panic and promptly lost her balance, both arms flying out instinctively as she stumbled on the thick branch. Her feet slipped, sending her backward, and she landed, quite neatly, in the fork between the tree trunk and a smaller branch. Her sketchbook and pencil spun to earth, papers flying in all directions.

"Oh my," the old lady exclaimed, setting her knitting aside and getting to her feet in a hurry. "Are you all right, dear?"

When she had come to her senses, Belle felt the flush race from her face down her neck. Regaining her balance, she mustered some dignity.

"I... I'm fine," she stuttered, collecting her wits as she climbed down the tree. Before she could reach the ground, the lady went about collecting the wayward papers. She stopped when she came to one sketch and brought it close to her face, narrowing her eyes.

"You don't have to do that," Belle panted, hastening her descent. "Please... it's okay. I'll get them."

Belle reached the ground and pushed through the creaky gate, in to the lush, green grounds of the park. The lady looked up from the piece of paper she held, a strange light in her eyes.

"Did you draw this?" she asked.

Belle flushed, seeing it was a sketch of the woman before her. "Yes," she admitted, hanging her head. "I'm sorry, I..."

"You shouldn't be," the woman said kindly, glancing from the drawing to Belle. The smile on her lips grew wistful. "It's lovely. You've got real talent."

Belle wondered if she was turning purple, her face burned so hot. "Thanks," she whispered. "Uh... I'm sorry I was watching you. I didn't mean... What I mean is, I was..."

"It's nothing to worry about, love," the woman assured her with a wave of her hand. "Can... can I keep this?"

Belle's jaw dropped. Relief swept over her when she realized she was not going to be in trouble, then elation at the thought that someone actually liked her drawing.

"Ah... sure. Of course you can."

"Thank you." The woman tucked the drawing in to her knitting bag as though it were something precious. "I've never seen... I mean, you made me look... Well," she chuckled then, looking embarrassed. "I've never taken a good photo. It's nice to see myself look half decent."

Belle beamed at the woman whose cheeks had become round and rosy. "It's my pleasure," she said softly.

# Chapter Two

"Look out, ding dong," a voice hollered at the same time something hard hit the back of Belle's head. Belle was thrown forward, the contents of her open water bottle spurting forth and drenching the front of her school dress.

"I *told* you to look out." Ben Carter sneered, collecting his ball and running an eye over Belle as if to admire his handiwork. When he saw her soaked dress his lips curved in a nasty smile.

"*Nice*, Ding Dong. It's a good look for you. Although somehow I doubt you'll be winning any wet t-shirt contests." Ben's beady eyes squeezed shut and his thick neck turned pink with raucous laughter. Mean girls extraordinaire, Anastasia and Brianna, who were standing nearby, erupted in to peals of giggles.

"You're not wrong." Brianna agreed, reclining against the canteen wall next to Anastasia. The pair of them bore a remarkable resemblance to models posing for a fashion shoot, which only added to the sting of Ben's words.

Belle cringed, feeling her face heat up and her heart begin to palpitate as she stood, transfixed to the spot, wondering whether to stand her ground or run like hell.

"Come on," Susie whispered, coming up alongside her and grabbing her by the elbow. There was irritation in her voice and Belle felt a twinge of hurt that even her best friend found her embarrassing. "Let's get you cleaned up."

In the bathroom, Susie slammed her hand against the button on the hand dryer and it roared to life. She instructed Belle to stand beneath it until her dress dried out.

"You really are a ding dong sometimes, you know that?" she muttered, sighing as she leant against the graffiti-covered bathroom wall. "It's like you don't want people to like you sometimes. Is that it? Well, I know *you're* more than happy spend your life alone but

I'd like to make at least *some* friends before my school life is officially over."

Belle felt the heat of frustration rising in her. "It's hardly my fault that Ben hit me in the back of the head with a ball." she protested, rubbing the spot that suddenly hurt at the reminder.

Susie sighed, frowning a little. "I guess not. But why didn't you just laugh or something? Make a joke out of it? You stood there like a stunned deer. Well...."

"What?"

Susie glanced at her, something close to pity in her eyes. Belle was suddenly aware that the only friend she had in the world had been growing increasingly annoyed with her lately. And she was starting to wonder whether it might not be more than a phase.

"Nothing," Susie sighed, glancing down at Belle's dress. "You're dry now. Let's go back out to lunch... or what's left of it."

Belle nodded, turning to inspect herself in the mirror. She looked all mottled and blotchy from the flush of humiliation and the heat of the dryer.

"Give me a minute."

"Sure," Susie shrugged as she turned and walked out the door.

Belle waited until Susie was out of sight. Then she ran in to one of the bathroom stalls, locked the door and sat down heavily on top of the toilet lid. With a deep, shuddering breath, she began to cry. When she was sick of her pitiful self, she got up to leave. "Sorry," she muttered as she bumped in to someone while trying to sneak out of the toilets. She kept her head down, only too aware of her puffy, red eyes and tearstained cheeks.

"Watch where you're going," a deep, male voice barked in exasperation.

Belle didn't recognize the voice and before she could stop herself she glanced up to see who it was. Her eyes widened as she found herself standing in the shadow of a tall, intimidating stranger. As she took in the boy's unmistakable good looks and air of quiet pride, she barely contained a gasp of surprise.

The boy's eyes ran over her and she could feel herself redden.

"Have you been crying?" he asked with disdain.

Belle stared at him, a thousand answers springing to mind but none of them coming out of her mouth. She managed to shake her head.

The boy narrowed his eyes. "Yeah, you have. Don't lie. Are you all right?"

She nodded dumbly. "Good. Then you can move out of my way, if you don't mind."

Belle found her voice as he was moving to pass her. He was so close that she could smell him, a dark, heady musk, and for a moment she forgot to move. His gaze locked with hers and for a second she was paralyzed as though she had fallen under a spell.

"Who are you?" she whispered, as she took in his gleaming, ice blue eyes and imposing mane of golden hair.

The boy raised his eyebrows and revealed a set of perfect, white teeth in a lazy smile. She had the unnerving suspicion that she was being examined.

"Your wildest dream, and your worst nightmare," he sneered.

Before she could catch her breath, he was gone.

# Chapter Three

Her mum didn't say a word when Belle skidded through the door at twenty-five past three. Mum pushed past on her way out and let the screen door slam shut behind her. Belle winced, glancing over apologetically at Sidney who merely shrugged and grinned at her.

"Don worry," he said. "Mum's tired. Got held up at work an coon't pick me up on time. Now she late fo her shift at the hospital. Yo know she don like to rush."

Belle didn't usually let her mother's moods get to her. Mum had every right to be moody. She worked two jobs: as a pharmacy assistant by day and a nurse by night to afford to pay for Sidney's various treatments, his wheelchair repayments and the expense of sending him to a school for children with special needs. She worked eleven hours most days and that didn't include the time spent caring for Sidney in between shifts and on weekends. On top of her small earnings, Sidney received a monthly disability payment, and there was the pittance from Belle's Sunday job. Yet, since their father had run off eighteen months after Sidney was born, money was tight all the time.

Despite Belle's best efforts, her mother's abrupt departure brought sudden tears to Belle's eyes.

"Beyya. Wot's wong?" Sidney asked, panicked.

"Nothing. Nothing Sid, it's okay. Don't worry. I'm fine." Belle blinked back her tears, wondering how she could possibly explain to a thirteen year old what it felt like to be humiliated by a half-wit football player, for her best friend to be embarrassed by her and to know in her heart that she would never measure up to the unreachable standards of beautiful people.

"Beyya, I know wen sumting's wong. Is it a boy? Is he dumb enough not to like you?"

Belle gave a hollow laugh. "No, it's not a boy," she sighed. Then she thought of the golden-haired stranger in the hallway and her stomach gave a little kick of protest. Maybe it was a boy, after all. A boy who, like all the others, would never look at her twice.

"Come on Beyya," Sidney pleaded, looking up at her with wet, brown eyes. Belle wondered whether, if she had been blessed with those dreamy eyes and luxurious, dark brown hair like the rest of her family, someone might actually look at her as something other than a gargantuan carrot-top freak.

"If it's okay with you, Sid," Belle forced a smile as she arranged Sidney's homework and laptop in front of him, "I think I'm going to lie down for a while. Call out if you need anything."

Sidney nodded, his eyes full of concern as Belle slunk out the door. She reached the sanctity of her room with a sigh of relief, flopped on to her bed and stared out the window at the magnificent maple tree that stood in the center of the yard. It was not yet autumn, but in time the golden leaves would turn a dazzling, ruby red, and blanket the ground with a velvet carpet come winter. When the last flame-colored leaf fell from its branches, it meant that winter had well and truly arrived.

Belle was comforted by that tree and remembered her grandmother. They had planted the tree to honor her memory and Belle still remembered pressing the seed in to the soft, brown soil when she was young.

"Arabella," her *máthair Chríona* used to say in her lilting Irish accent whenever Belle complained about her crimson curls. She could recall the feel of the supple leaf against her palm as *máthair Chríona* handed it to her. "Your hair is a gift. It is the color of the maple leaf before winter. In the land of your ancestors, such hair foretells of great fire within, and of great strength and inner beauty. You are destined to change lives, my dear. Of that, you can be sure."

Belle lifted a strand of her hair and coiled it around her index finger. The color was startling against her pale skin. For a moment it almost looked as though her finger was bleeding. Belle grimaced and flung the repulsive strand aside. She had clung to *máthair Chríona's* stories as a child, desperate to believe that someday things would be different, that the fire within her would reveal itself. She remembered huddling in her grandmother's lap after the kids at school had tormented her, asking her to tell her the same story over and over. But as she grew older and *máthair Chríona* passed away, the memories faded and Belle remained shy, clumsy and ostracized.

That she was destined to change lives seemed less and less probable. And yet the dream of it never fully perished.

# Chapter Four

"What's he like?" Susie exclaimed, clasping her hands under her chin as Belle took a seat beside her in class. Belle was surprised to be greeted with such enthusiasm.

"Who?"

"*Who, who*?" Susie hooted, rolling her eyes. "Are you serious? Noah Cole. What's he like? I saw you talking to him yesterday at lunch."

Belle realized who Susie was talking about. So the golden haired boy's name was Noah Cole. It sounded almost regal.

"What happened to you yesterday, anyhow? After you were with Noah you ran off and I didn't see you for the rest of lunch."

"Oh." Belle hesitated, not feeling like sharing the fact that she'd fled and hid in the library until the bell rang.

"Never mind. Anyway, tell me. What's he like? What did he say to you? I want to know everything."

"There's nothing to tell," Belle lowered her voice as Mr. Whitworth, their Visual Arts teacher, entered the classroom. "I ran in to him as I was coming out of the bathroom. I said I was sorry and he told me to watch where I was going."

Susie made a disgusted sound. "That'd be right," she muttered. "Trust you to ruin your chances with a guy right off the bat."

Belle sighed. "Actually, I think it was his fault. He was pretty rude. And he was walking really fast, right past the bathroom doorway and…"

"Shh." Susie hissed and when Belle looked up she understood why she had been shushed. Noah Cole stood in the doorway of room 206 leaning against the frame with a black bag slung over one shoulder. His presence was arresting, those piercing blue eyes and mane of golden hair attracting more than a few stares. This time, Belle could see how tall he was, how immaculately dressed and self-assured he seemed. And she noticed other things, like the slightly petulant protrusion of his lower lip and the bored, distant look in his eyes.

"Wow," Susie murmured, but Belle found herself much less impressed with him than she had been the first time. "You realize who he is, don't you? That's him. He's the orphan."

"*What*?" Belle whispered harshly but she was cut short when Mr. Whitworth began speaking.

"Welcome to the first art class for year twelve." he said brightly, addressing the thirteen students who comprised half of the entire grade. "Your last year at Pitts High. I'll bet most of you are cheering." He smiled as Ben Carter and his sidekick Daniel Woodhouse sniggered and then he noticed Noah in the doorway. "Ah, Mr. Cole, you made it. Wonderful. I trust that everyone will make you feel welcome. So, son, are you enjoying Pitts so far?"

Belle couldn't take her eyes off Noah. *This* was the boy who had lost his mother. He was a far cry from the orphan she had imagined. He didn't remotely resemble a withdrawn, pitiable creature cowering somewhere in a corner.

When he made no attempt to respond, Mr. Whitworth said gently, "You can take a seat, mate. Anywhere is fine."

Belle liked Mr. Whitworth. As well as teaching her favorite subject, he was a warm, good-natured sort with a sense of humor, unlike most of the teachers at Pitts. He encouraged her passion for drawing in a way that no one else had, and when she was in his classes she could almost imagine that she actually mattered.

But Noah barely acknowledged him. He sauntered through the room and took a seat at the back table without making eye contact with anyone. Belle watched him with a morbid sense of curiosity. She couldn't help but notice that all the female heads turned in his direction as he passed. Some of the boys looked too but with scorn more so than admiration. Belle wondered if perhaps they felt as intimidated as she did.

"OMG, he is *so* hot." Susie whispered urgently, her breath tickling Belle's ear. "What are the chances of a guy like that landing in *Pitts*?"

Belle ignored her best friend. Her head was swimming. Noah's words echoed in her mind. *"I'm your wildest dream, and your worst nightmare."* What a weird thing to say to a total stranger. Or to anyone. And what exactly was it supposed to mean? Belle felt unsettled being in the same room as Noah Cole.

"Your first task for the year is a relatively simple one, and one I'm sure you'll all enjoy." Mr. Whitworth was speaking again and Belle forced herself to concentrate. He smiled widely, gesturing to some sketchpads and a collection of graphite pencils and charcoal arranged on his desk.

"We'll call it drawing one-o-one, hey?" he chuckled and a few students made a token attempt at joining in, but most only groaned. Belle felt a flutter of anticipation in her stomach. "Come on, kids, not many people get to spent forty-five minutes of their day drawing pictures. Wait 'til you're out in the real world. You get fired for that kind of thing." This was met with more groans, but Mr. Whitworth only laughed.

"I want you to find partners. No wait, scratch that," he amended, glancing over at Ben and Daniel who were sitting with the mean girls. "You're going to be *allocated* partners. No boyfriend and girlfriend pairs. No friendship pairs. We're going to do this thing properly. I want you to experience seeing someone in a different light. I want you to draw each other. And I mean *really* draw each other. With great care and attention to detail. This is a task that we're going to be coming back to throughout the semester. You will need to do several drafts and experiment with various techniques and medium before you attempt your final work. I want you to create a raw, honest portrait of someone in this class. Someone you don't know well. But, seeing as this assignment will require you to meet outside of school as well, maybe in a few months you will."

A unanimous moan went through the room and the excited flutter in Belle's stomach became a swarm of bees. She was going to be expected to talk to someone? To spend time with them? To look at them closely and to let them look at *her*? She started to feel sick.

"Oh, by the way," Mr. Whitworth went on as he handed out the drawing material. "The best work will be entered in to the annual competition at the Pitts Town Centre Art Gallery during the art festival at the end of the year. And the winner of that competition is up for some substantial prize money. Ten thousand dollars to be exact."

A murmur went through the class and Belle felt an unmistakable tug as she considered what she could do with such a sum of money.

"As some of you may know, some prominent artists, curators and art dealers often scout these kinds of events for talent so it's possible a budding artist might land their big break. So for those of you interested," he glanced at Belle meaningfully, "the opportunity is there. Let's get cracking."

Amid the sighs and moans, Mr. Whitworth made a show of taking the roll from his top drawer and brandishing it as though it contained that year's best actor nominations. With a smirk, he cleared his throat and proceeded to call out names two at a time, pairing each student with the person who would be their drawing partner for the entire semester.

Susie looked almost as nervous as Belle felt. Her eyes darted anxiously as each name was crossed off the list, leaving fewer and fewer potential partners. Soon there were only six students remaining. Belle, Susie, Brianna, Brenton Jones who was a Canadian exchange student who started at Pitts the previous year, John Cornwell, a tall, thin, bookish sort of boy who Belle suspected Susie had a crush on. And Noah Cole.

Belle's heart rammed against her ribs as if trying to escape. When Susie's name was called she jumped. But soon Susie was giggling when she was paired with John.

Belle's ears were roaring as the next two names were called out. Brianna and Brenton. Brianna and Brenton. Brianna and Brenton. Time seemed to stand still. Then her gaze shot to the back of the room and locked with a pair of ice blue eyes.

Mr. Whitworth's next words sounded like they were being shouted through a megaphone in to Belle's disbelieving ears.

"Noah Cole and Arabella Quinn."

# Chapter Five

"Let's get this over with," Noah said in a cool voice, eyeing Belle with barely disguised contempt. "You're not going to cry on me today, are you?"

Belle gaped in shock as they descended the narrow stairwell and Noah laughed. It was a hollow sound that made Belle's skin crawl.

"Don't look so horrified. It was a joke. I'd have thought a redhead would be used to that by now. Speaking of which, is your hair natural? God, I hope so. You'd want to hope *that* didn't happen on purpose."

Belle shook her head, stunned by his words. He didn't know her from Eve and he was already mocking her. What was it about her that invited such scorn?

"Yes, it's natural." Belle replied..

Noah didn't respond. It was as though he'd already become bored by the conversation. He sat down on one of the wooden seats at the far end of the playground and flipped open his sketchbook.

"So, where do we start, red? Or is it ding dong they call you? Clever bunch, aren't they? Ding dong Belle. Hilarious." He looked up at her impassively, his face appearing a little drawn, and Belle wondered if he was tired. It was then that she noticed something about the way Noah spoke. It was distinctly different to the dialect of the people she'd grown up with. His words were more carefully chosen, his annunciation clear and his voice smooth, devoid of harsh, nasal edges. It wasn't quite a British accent, but it was close.

"I think I prefer red," Noah mused, seeming to have forgotten that he had asked a question. "You couldn't get that color out of a bottle. Arabella is your name, correct? Redbella. Yes, I think that nickname suits you."

Belle decided there was no possible way to respond to that. She sat down awkwardly on the other end of the wooden seat and opened her own sketchbook. She stared at the blank page, waiting for some divine power to tell her what to do next.

When she lifted her gaze, Noah was staring at her face, his steely eyes looking as though they might bore straight through her. Belle started in surprise and dropped her pencil. She bent to retrieve it and when she straightened up Noah smiled at her. It was that same slow, lazy smile she had seen the day before and it made her feel uneasy, like he knew something that she didn't. Like she was a bug under a microscope and he could crush her at any moment if he chose to, and they both knew it.

"Relax, red," Noah said evenly, regarding her through sleepy lids. "I'm observing the subject matter. That hair's going to be hard to draw. But you're features are plain enough so it shouldn't be too much of a challenge."

Belle cleared her throat and poised her pencil above her sketchbook. *Plain*, he'd called her. Well, it could have been worse. As she was about to touch pencil to paper, Noah piped up again.

"So have you lived in this dump of a town all your life? I mean, I've only been here two days and I'm already suicidal. How do you do it?"

Belle looked at him, wondering whether it was a serious question or if he was trying to get a rise out of her.

"Yes. I uh… I grew up here. I've never lived anywhere else."

Noah snorted. "Figures. If you've never known anything else, you'd have no idea how common everyone is around here. It'd be funny if it wasn't so depressing."

Belle stared at her lap again. Why was he bothering to talk to her if he was going to be rude? "Where are you from?" she asked in an attempt to change the subject.

"Sydney. Kirribilli, actually. Have you heard of it? Probably not. I'm sure you've never even stepped foot out of Pitts. It's near the harbor. Not a bad place to be when the New Year's fireworks go off." He shrugged, spinning a graphite pencil between his fingers.

"Have you always lived there?"

"Of course not," Noah scoffed. "We have a place in the country, and a place on the coast. That's where I'm staying now. I lived in France for a year, in Dubai for six months, China for a while… I can't remember how long. We have a place in Wimbledon where I spend every summer. And we lived in New York when I was about three, though I can't really remember it. You know, the usual."

The usual? Belle thought in amazement. What was usual about living in so many different countries before the age of eighteen? What was usual about a family owning so many international properties? It certainly explained Noah's accent.

"Oh," was all she said.

Noah chuckled, looking smug. "There are some benefits to having a father who was an international journalist, I suppose. It was easy enough for him to fly us around all expenses paid, and I'm an only child. He was at the top of his game by the age of thirty. Austin Cole, have you heard of him?"

Belle was surprised that she had. When she was a child, Austin Cole was a household name. She could recall seeing him on the television almost daily. He was the one who reported the 9/11 attacks as they happened. Though she was too young to remember it at the time, she'd seen the footage on some documentary only a few weeks ago.

"How old are you?" she asked suddenly as something occurred to her.

Noah looked at her, a frown creasing his brow. "I'll be eighteen in June," he said slowly. "Why?"

Belle did a quick subtraction in her head and gasped. "You were there when it happened? In New York?"

Understanding dawned in Noah's eyes. He pursed his lips and frowned. "Yes. I was there. Dad was stationed in New York on business. We lived there for about four months. We were ten blocks away when the planes hit."

Belle's eyes grew wide. What an amazing and terrifying thing for a child to have witnessed.

"Anyway, we were all fine," Noah said, waving a dismissive hand. "I was so young, I don't really remember it. And I'm here, aren't I? No big deal."

Belle couldn't help but think that while Noah was here, his parents no longer were. Clearly, he had been through a lot in his short life and then he had been orphaned to boot. All the money in the world could never compensate for that.

Sympathy pawed at Belle's stomach and she wished she could think of something to say. A shadow passed over them as a nearby tree swayed in the wind and she suddenly noticed that the sun had sunk quite low in the western sky.

"What time is it?" she asked quickly, realizing she had forgotten to wear a watch.

"Why? Have you got somewhere better to be, red?"

"No… yes. I mean… could you tell me the time? Please?" Belle hated to beg, but if she was late again, her mother was going to kill her.

Noah looked primed to refuse her request. Then he glanced at her hands and saw that they were twitching in her lap.

"It's ten past three," he drawled eventually, holding up his wrist to reveal an expensive looking watch.

"Crap." Belle exclaimed, jumping to her feet and shoving her things in to her backpack. It was a pain having outdoor sessions in the last period of the day as the school bell couldn't be heard from the far end of the playground. "I've got to go. I'm sorry. Um… thank you. For…for the time. For today. I'll see you later." She slung her backpack over her shoulder and started running down the grassy slope as fast as she could.

"Hey, red." she heard Noah call out from behind her. "You forgot something."

Belle paused and glanced over her shoulder though she didn't have a moment to spare.

"What?"

That slow smile emerged again. "You forgot to thank me for my awesome company."

Belle stared at him for a full three seconds without blinking. Then she shook her head, turned and bolted across the playground, only too aware of how ridiculous she must have looked with her beanpole legs pumping and her red locks flying.

It occurred to her half way through her six-block sprint that neither of them had started their sketches that afternoon.

# Chapter Six

*A double period of Art* was all Belle could think as she paced the corridor outside room 206, waiting for Susie to arrive. How was she ever going to survive it?

Susie appeared at a quarter to nine, her eyes bright and her cheeks flushed from climbing the stairs. They always met before school, even if they weren't in the same class. It had been that way since they were in year seven.

Though theirs had been a friendship borne primarily of convenience, Belle and Susie had some things in common. They were the only two students in the grade who had graduated from primary school with a ninth grade reading level. They were two of the few Pitts residents who aspired to become anything other than a football player, a beautician or a pub owner. So, despite the divide that had grown between them of late, Belle was relieved that Susie was keeping to their unspoken tradition, despite the fact that Belle suspected it had more to do with Noah than with their friendship.

"So, how was it?" Susie panted, smoothing down her shiny black hair and straightening her glasses. Belle smiled, thinking that sometimes it was nice that her friend was so predictable.

"How was what?" Belle asked acting obtuse, and Susie made a frustrated sound.

"Don't play coy, Quinn. You know exactly what. Now spill."

Belle bit her lip as she tried to think of a way to explain the strangeness of her afternoon with Noah.

"It was okay, I guess."

"Okay? You spent the afternoon with a guy who looks like a movie star, for God's sake. You didn't fall over or anything, did you?"

"No," Belle rolled her eyes. "No, we talked. Sort of. I mean, I still think he's rude. He's unbelievably arrogant. But he's led a fascinating life."

A few students began to file through the corridor and Belle and Susie had to move to get out of their way.

"And? What does that mean? What qualifies as fascinating?"

Belle shrugged. "He's lived in a lot of different countries. I noticed he's got a strange sort of accent, which makes sense, since he's lived all over, I guess. He was in New York when the September eleven attacks happened."

"What?" Susie's eyes popped. "Wow. Oh yeah, that's right. His dad was Austin Cole. I remember him. I remember seeing that old documentary with him in it the other week.

"Yeah, me too. And to think Noah was there."

"Yeah," Susie breathed, sighing wistfully. "It's pretty amazing. I wonder what on earth a guy like that is doing in this dump? Do you think maybe he's staying with family or something? I mean, otherwise wouldn't you think he'd go to a private school?"

"I have no idea," Belle replied honestly.

"Well, you have to promise to find out as much as you can. I mean you're partners with him, you have to make the most of it while you can, all right?"

Belle rolled her eyes. "Sure, Susie. I'll bring a note pad and a list of questions next time."

"Wait a minute," Susie interrupted in a hushed voice. "I think he's coming. Act natural."

As Belle turned her head, Noah appeared at the top of the stairwell. Susie fell silent and Belle stiffened, preparing to avoid his piercing ice blue gaze. Noah wasn't alone. Anastasia Asquith walked beside him, her long, blonde hair swinging about her shoulders, a flirtatious glint in her eye as she glanced up at him through her lashes and giggled. They looked achingly beautiful together. Noah's tall, broad frame perfectly shadowed Anna's petite dancer's body. Noah was wearing the same bored expression Belle had seen the previous day but she thought she caught a little smile cross his lips as he passed by.

"Typical," Susie said bitterly as she watched them enter the classroom. "They're such an obvious pair it's almost disgusting. Come on, Belle. I guess we'd better head in."

\*\*\*

"I'm going to sleep with her, you know."

"Excuse me?" Belle shot Noah a startled look from her cross-legged position on the ground beneath a gum tree. Her blank sketchbook sat untouched in front of her.

"You heard me. I'm going to sleep with Anastasia. I'm not sure when yet. But soon."

Belle blinked at him. "Oh," was all she could manage. "That's, um, nice."

Noah laughed. "You don't think it's *nice*, red. You need to start telling the truth."

Belle sighed. At the rate they were going, they were never going to get started on their assignment. She wondered if Noah had ever had to do any work in his life or if everything had always been handed to him on a silver platter.

"What do you want me to say, then?" she asked, looking up at him. As soon as she did so, she knew it was a mistake. Those steely eyes captured her and wouldn't let go.

"I want you to be honest. I want to know what you really think."

Belle looked down and gave a shrug. Why on earth would he care what she thought about him sleeping with the bimbo of Pitts High? They barely knew each other. "I don't know what I think. I don't think anything about it, I guess."

"Yes, you do," he goaded. "You do and you're not telling. You're so used to no one listening to anything you say that you've stopped bothering."

Belle looked at him sharply but he merely smiled his lazy smile. "I get bored a lot," he said by way of explanation. "It amuses me to analyze people. I think I've got you pegged."

Belle felt a twinge of anger at his audacity and something else she couldn't quite define. It had been a long time since anyone had commented on anything about her aside from her glaring imperfections.

"Don't worry, red. Your secret's safe with me." He grinned at her and Belle tried hard not to stare at him. He was beautiful to look at and yet what lay beneath infuriated her beyond reason. She felt like she was being driven mad.

Noah spun the pencil he held between his fingers until it became a blur. "Most girls would think the same as you. That I'm doing something underhanded. That I have an unfair advantage in the game. But the girls as willing as I am. And it's crazy fun, red. You have no idea." He laughed but there was no real humor in the sound.

Belle found herself watching him. It wasn't attraction she felt, or pity, but something halfway between the two.

"Do you want to know how I do it?" Noah wiggled his eyebrows. "How I perform the art of seduction?"

Belle stared at her lap, fiddling with the hem of her school dress. "No. Not really."

"Come on, red. Don't play games. I know you're wondering."

Belle clenched her hands in little fists. "I don't play games. And I don't need to wonder. It's obvious."

Noah's sharp laughter startled her. "Is it? I didn't realize it was obvious. But if that's the case, why don't you explain it to me?"

Belle hesitated. She didn't want to feed his already inflated ego and provide him with more fuel to ridicule her. Wringing her hands, she chose her next words carefully.

"Girls like you," she said simply, getting to her feet for something to do and brushing the dirt from her uniform. To her chagrin, Noah stood as well. "You're… you're charming, I guess. When you're not being rude and arrogant. You're confident. Flirtatious. You're good looking." Belle took a shaky breath. "That's hardly an art. As I said, it's obvious."

Noah was silent for a moment. Then his crocodile smile widened and he took a swift step closer to her, leaning in to invade her personal space.

"Good looking, huh? Charming and confident. Why, red, I didn't know you felt that way."

Belle took a step backward, narrowing her eyes. "I don't. I'm stating facts."

"Tsk tsk, now you're back to your lies again. I don't buy it, red." He closed the distance she had placed between them and whispered close to her ear. Belle shivered despite herself. "Don't think I'm going to let you off that easily. Don't think I haven't noticed the way you are around me. How nervous you get, and the way your heart beats faster when I'm close to you."

Belle jumped as his fingers brushed her throat in a feather-light touch and she heard him chuckle. There was no way he could mistake the feel of her pulse racing beneath her skin.

"It's okay," he breathed, pulling back so that his face was inches from hers. "It's natural to feel that way. I feel it too. Did you know that, red?"

Heat swept upward from Belle's chest and she suddenly felt feverish. What was happening? What was he doing?

Noah's ice blue eyes burned as she stared up at him in wonder. And before she could draw breath he was leaning in, ever so slowly, bringing his lips so near to hers that she could feel his breath on her face. Belle closed her eyes.

A short silence was followed by a bark of laughter and Belle's eyes snapped open, jolting her back to consciousness. Noah was standing at a fair distance, watching her with cool amusement in his eyes. He shook his head.

"That was almost too easy," he sneered. "It proved my point rather nicely though, didn't it? Honestly, red. Did you really think I was going to kiss you?"

Belle's face flushed so violently it almost caught fire. Her ears began to roar as she became painfully aware that she had fallen victim to a horrible, malicious prank. She had never felt so mortified. And for Arabella Quinn, that was saying something.

"You look like you've seen a ghost, red. Come on, it was only a joke," Noah stepped toward her and Belle took a step back, tripping over a thatch of grass to add to her humiliation.

"Don't touch me," she whispered fiercely, tears of anger burning her eyes. Before they could break forth, she turned from Noah and stumbled down the hill.

She didn't stop running until she got home.

# Chapter Seven

The house was empty when Belle arrived and she was deeply grateful for it. Rarely did she have the chance to be alone. Her time was spent either at school, with Sidney, or working at the pharmacy on Sundays, so a moment's peace was something to be savored.

Belle threw herself on her bed and let the tears flow freely. She sobbed until her stomach hurt and her head ached, and when she thought she had finished she cried some more.

A while later, as she lay staring at the ceiling, the horrible reality dawned on her. She had skipped school. She had run out of class at ten o'clock in the morning. Everyone would notice she was missing. She had left her bag behind for God's sake. Noah would no doubt have told everyone what had happened and they would all be laughing at her expense by now.

Belle rolled on to her stomach and moaned. How had this happened? The humiliation was acute, slicing through her as she re-lived Noah's cruel prank over and over in her mind. How stupid she had been to think for even a second that he was going to kiss her. How was she ever going to live it down? She never wanted to show her face at school again.

Noah Cole was a bastard. The truth of it was pure and simple. He was wretched and selfish and had used her for his own amusement. Had he not wounded her, she might have pitied him. But how could she pity someone who was so bored with life that he resorted to manipulating others as a form of sport?

Belle had no idea which path to choose. If she requested another partner for the project, everyone would want to know why. All the students were already paired up, so that meant she would have to swap partners with someone and, unlike her and Noah, they had probably already started their work. And there was no way she could change subjects, not when there was the opportunity to have her work entered in the annual Pitts Art Gallery competition. Not when ten thousand dollars and her possible future in the art world was at stake.

But if she continued working with Noah, she'd have to see him again. Twice a week. Until the end of semester, which was five months away. It was unthinkable.

"Is that you, Bels?" she heard her mother's voice calling from the hallway.

Belle jerked upright with a gasp. In a nanosecond, she was scrambling across the bed towards the box of tissues that sat on her bedside table. She yanked out a handful of them and began wiping her eyes and face furiously.

"Belle?" Her mum stuck her head around the door and for a moment Belle felt like she was looking in a mirror. Her Mum was in bad shape. Her eyes looked swollen, her nose was pink and she seemed drawn and tired.

"Mum, are you all right?"

"No. I'm sick." Mum croaked, leaning heavily against the doorframe. She raked a hand through her thick, wavy brown hair. "Work sent me home. Which is ridiculous because they need me and they don't have a replacement." She coughed noisily and heaved a great sigh. "You don't look so good yourself, Bels. What are you doing home from school?"

"Free period," Belle said quickly, the lie coming to her in a flash.

Mum frowned, rubbing her nose with a crinkled tissue. "At this time? It's what, ten thirty?"

"Yeah. I came back to, uh, to work on my art project."

Mum's gaze fell on the handful of tissues Belle was clutching and she narrowed her eyes.

"Arabella. Is everything all right?"

The phone rang at that moment and mother and daughter locked gazes. Belle knew it was only a matter of time before she lost the battle of wills so she gritted her teeth, willing her mother to walk out the door and answer the phone.

After three rings, Mum sighed and looked away, forfeiting the contest. "Can you get that, darl? I can hardly talk."

"Sure," Belle jumped up, thankful for an excuse to leave. She squeezed past Mum and dashed down the hallway and in to the tiny kitchen, picking up the receiver on the sixth ring.

"Hello?"

"Belle? It's Susie."

Belle cringed. "Oh. Hey. What's up?"

"Are you okay?"

"Uh, yeah. Yeah, I'm okay. Where are you?"

"At school, dummy. It's recess and I'm using the office phone. Mrs. Bowser said it was all right."

"Oh." Neither Susie nor Belle's families could afford to give them mobile phones, so it was no surprise that Susie had gone to the office to call her.

"Thank God you're okay. After class I couldn't find you so I asked around and Mr. Whitworth said you went home. Noah said you were really sick or something. You seemed all right this morning. Did something happen?"

Belle felt a strange tingle in her chest. Noah had covered for her? Why would he do that when he could have told on her, humiliating her further? Wasn't that what he wanted?

"Belle? Hello?"

Belle sighed. "No. I mean, yeah. Kind of. I mean, I am sick." She forced a cough to prove the lie. "Mum's got it too. But Noah made things worse. He was…" She trailed off, wondering if she should bite the bullet and be honest.

"He what? Spit it out, Quinn."

"He's horrible, Susie." Belle burst out, blinking back tears as she admitted the bitter truth.

"What? Horrible? Are you kidding?"

Belle wiped her nose with the scrunched up tissues she'd shoved in her pocket. "No, I'm not kidding. He's horrible. I don't want to be partners with him anymore."

"What? Why? What did he say?"

Belle went silent. She was pretty sure Susie would find a way to blame her if she told her what had happened.

"Come on Bels. It can't have been that horrible. You were the one saying how sad it was and that we should all be feeling sorry for him. He was orphaned. He can't be that bad. He can't be any worse than what you're used to with Ben."

Belle knew that what Susie was saying made sense. Belle knew Noah must be in pain. She knew she should be feeling sorry for him. And she had been putting up with taunts and jibes from the boys at school since day one. But she also knew that this was different. How could she explain to Susie that while Ben had tortured her for years, in the end he was a big, dumb, fat-necked football player. His insults were half-baked at best. Belle didn't really care what Ben Carter thought.

But Noah Cole was something else entirely. He was intelligent, sophisticated and cunning. He could take one look at her and know all her deepest secrets. Noah Cole was dangerous.

"I guess not," Belle heard herself lie.

"And although you know I'd kill to swap with you, John and I have already started our portraits. Mine's really good so far so I don't want to have to start again. And the one he's done of me makes me look pretty cute." She giggled and Belle took it as a sign that Susie and John were getting along rather nicely. She felt a pang of jealousy followed by a stab of sudden panic.

There was no way out.

Belle tried desperately to think of a plan of escape, of any possible course of action that would get her out of having to work with Noah. She could drop out of school. Run away. Jump off a cliff. Join the circus. Anything was better than having to face him again.

"So, I'll see you tomorrow then? Do you think you'll be better?"

Belle's stomach sank as she realized she had no choice. There was nothing she could do. There was no alternative.

"Yeah," she murmured, giving up. "I'll be fine."

# Chapter Eight

"I can't afford to get sick," Mum moaned, holding her head in her hands as she sat at the breakfast table. "Who's going to take care of Sid? How're we going to get him to and from school?"

"I'll drive him," Belle piped up, eager for a chance to use the car. It would mean escaping school early that afternoon.

Daisy moaned again. "You only got your license, Bels. It's not safe. Besides, it'll make you late for school."

"Well, what alternative do you have?" Belle reasoned, watching as her brother spooned some soggy cereal in to his mouth, half of it dribbling down his chin. "It's not like we can pay for a taxi. If I leave now I'll have plenty of time, and I can finish school a little early to pick him up if you write me a note."

Mum looked primed to play the battle of wills again but then she threw her hands up in defeat. "Oh, all right." She sighed loudly, making a show of coughing and spluttering and blowing her nose. Though she hated to admit she was wrong, Daisy Quinn could never argue with logic.

"Yay," Sidney exclaimed, banging his hands against his walker tray in delight. Splodges of cereal sprung from the bowl and seemed to hover in the air above Sid's head for a second before landing with a wet *thwack* in his hair. Mum and Belle stared at him in stunned silence for a moment and then, despite herself, Belle burst out laughing.

\*\*\*

"Here's your bag," a deep voice said from behind her and Belle jumped. She knew who it was at once. Her body went rigid and she wished that she could become invisible or sink unnoticed through the hallway floor. "You left it when you scampered off yesterday. I thought you might be needing it."

When she didn't move, Noah stepped forward in one swift movement to stand before her, holding out her backpack like he was dangling a bone in front of a hungry dog. Belle glanced around nervously but no one was paying them any notice.

When she dared to look at him, Noah was closer than expected, his eyes seeming darker than their usual ice blue. Warmer somehow. She shivered at his nearness and the dark, musky smell of his skin, but the pleasure quickly dissolved to shame. Her cheeks flamed as she re-lived the previous morning yet again and she dropped her gaze to stare at her shoes.

"Don't be mad, red." Noah's voice was smooth and held a note of regret. Whether it was false or not, Belle couldn't tell. "I'm sorry I tricked you. It was only a joke. I didn't mean to upset you."

Belle realized then that she could choose to let him win by revealing how much he'd hurt her or she could show him that he didn't matter to her in the slightest, and that he was nowhere near as powerful as he thought he was. That they could go on with their lives.

Belle lifted her chin and forced a smile. "It's okay. I wasn't feeling well yesterday. I'm much better now."

Noah surveyed her coolly. If he was thinking of calling her bluff, he decided against it. "I'm glad. I wouldn't want a fearsome redhead coming after me." He chuckled and reached out to grasp a tendril of her hair between his thumb and forefinger. Belle watched, mesmerized, as he ran it slowly between his fingers then let it fall back against her arm.

"Anyway, I wanted to give this back." He dropped the bag next to her left leg, smirked, and sauntered away.

***

Something strange was happening in math class. And not the usual kind of strangeness Belle experienced when her daydreaming was interrupted and the teacher asked her what pi equalled, but something else. Something new.

"Hey ding dong," Anastasia's high-pitched voice filtered in to her thoughts. "Ding Dong, wake up. Are you okay?"

Belle blinked and her eyes focused on Anastasia's angelic face. She was peering at her with her long-lashed baby blues, her smooth brow furrowed with concern. Did Anastasia Asquith ask if Belle was okay? She wondered if she had heard right.

"Huh? Yeah. Yeah I'm okay."

"You sure?" Anastasia asked sweetly. "You're looking a little pale. I mean, more than usual."

Belle shifted her gaze to the floor, awaiting the inevitable joke or insult. Was that it? She looked a little more pale than usual? Anastasia could do better than that. But she didn't say anything more. After several moments had passed, Belle slowly raised her head. When Anastasia caught her eye and smiled Belle nearly died of shock.

Later that day, as Belle was re-filling her water bottle at the drinking fountain, something hard impacted with the back of her left leg. It startled her and stung a lot, but Belle pretended she hadn't felt it, knowing that if she turned around she was only inviting her assailant to ridicule her.

"Sorry, ding dong." Ben Carter's raspy voice called out from behind her.

Sorry? Belle thought in amazement. Was he serious?

Suddenly Ben was beside her, eyeing her as if to admire his handiwork, as he always did. Only he wasn't laughing. He picked up the ball and tucked it under one arm. "Didn't drench ya this time." He smiled. "Cool. Well, see ya, Belle."

Belle watched him walk off to join his friends, her eyes nearly bulging out of her head. Ben Carter had called her Belle. He had actually called her by her real name. She saw Daniel come up beside him and nudge him in the side. "What was that about?" he asked, sounding as amazed as Belle felt.

Ben shrugged. "I'm not in to that bullshit anymore," he said carelessly.

"You're not? Why?"

"I dunno. Ben said...Ow. Jeez, Anna, what'd you do that for?"

Brianna had kicked him in the shin before he could finish his sentence.

"Shut *up*," she muttered, glancing over her shoulder at Belle. Their eyes met and Brianna smiled and gave a wink. Belle had to hold on the edge of the drinking fountain to stop herself from falling over.

# Chapter Nine

When Belle arrived at Sidney's school that afternoon, one of his teachers was there to greet her at the door.

"You must be Belle," she smiled warmly. "It's lovely too finally meet you. I'm Mrs. Stevens. Sid's very excited that you're picking him up today."

Belle smiled, blushing a little. "Yeah, he was pretty excited about it this morning."

"Well, you're a good sister to take care of him so well. Now, I don't want you to worry, but he's been a little under the weather this afternoon," Mrs. Stevens said, leaning closer and speaking in a low voice as if she didn't want anyone to overhear.

"Is he okya?" Belle asked quickly, immediately on alert.

"Yes, yes, sweetie, he's fine, I promise. We would have called if it were urgent. He's been very tired this afternoon. He didn't eat much at lunch and he fell asleep in his chair during our last session. He's only woken up now."

Belle nodded, relieved that it didn't seem to be anything serious. Without being able to get much exercise, Sidney's body was weak and he was susceptible to almost any bug that went around, so hearing that he was "under the weather" made her think he had come down with Mum's flu.

Belle followed Mrs. Stevens in to the classroom and saw Sidney sitting by the window in his walker, looking rumpled and half asleep. When he saw Belle he smiled.

"Beyya. You made it. Howwas yo day?"

Belle shook her head. "Never mind that, little bro, what's going on with you? Mrs. Stevens said you're not feeling well?"

Sid shook his head vigorously. "I fine, Beyya, I fine, I pomise. I just tired, thass all."

"All right buddy, well we'd better get you home then, okay?

Sidney nodded and Belle gave him a kiss on the cheek and began wheeling him to the car.

With her brother in the back and the breeze on her face, Belle felt a sense of freedom that was rare in her world. She wondered if maybe she could start taking Sidney to and from school more often, if her mother might allow it on afternoons when she had a free period so she could leave school a little earlier. It would help Mum out and it would mean that for a short time Belle could feel as though she was escaping her dreary little life.

With the wind in her hair, her music playing on the radio and that fluttery feeling of possibility, Belle could almost believe that someday things might be different.

***

The following Tuesday, her classmates were still acting strangely. As she waited for Noah, who was running late, she kept catching smiles from Anastasia and Brianna from across the room. Belle was so confused that she didn't know how to respond. She had always wondered what it would be like if the popular kids stopped making fun of her, if they grew out of their prejudice and started seeing her as a person. But the sudden, bizarre switch in behavior was more unsettling than anything else.

Noah arrived and a murmur ran through the class. Belle saw Anastasia wave to him and Brianna turn her head and giggle. Noah smiled cordially and turned straight to Belle, winking at her and beckoning for her to follow him. With a glance around the room at all the awed faces, she started to get a slinking feeling she might know what was going on after all. "So," Noah said as they sat at their regular seat. As usual, there was no one around save for a few students from their art class at the other end of the playground. "Are you still mad at me, red, or have I redeemed myself?"

Belle watched him carefully as he spoke. His eyes were twinkling and the golden strands of his hair glinted in the afternoon sun. A soft smile barely touched his lips as he looked at her expectantly. In a short time, Belle had figured out that nothing was as it seemed with Noah Cole. He was always up to something and he was always one step ahead. She wasn't sure she was quick enough to keep up.

"I'm not mad," she said honestly, that feeling having passed days ago. "I want to get to work, that's all. Everyone else has started already and I don't want to get left behind."

"Don't you like talking to me, red? I'm crushed." Noah clutched his hands to his chest as though he had been wounded.

Belle didn't bite. She kept her nerve and looked him in the eye. "It's not that. As I said, I want to get to work. I don't know about you, but I'd like at least a chance of getting in to the art exhibition this year."

Noah lowered his hands and regarded her coolly. He picked up a pencil and began spinning it between his fingers. "From what I can see, you don't need much practice. With your talent I'd say you could churn out a first rate portrait in minutes."

Belle narrowed her eyes, wondering what he was getting at this time. Couldn't he speak like a normal person? Why did he have to talk in riddles?

"You do recall that I had your bag in my possession for an evening, don't you? Didn't it occur to you that I might have been.... curious?"

Belle's heart gave a little kick. He hadn't. He wouldn't. "You went through my things?" she spluttered, trying to keep her voice calm.

"I've already told you I get bored. I would have thought you'd suspect, but never mind. I don't see why you should care, really. Your drawings are quite good. I'd go so far as to say they're more than good, in fact. And you can't think you'll ever get anywhere with them if they're always hidden away."

Belle's hands were clenched in little fists. She felt as though she was being wrenched in two different directions, indignation at having had her privacy invaded and elation at someone appreciating her work.

"And I don't hear you thanking me for calling the dogs off, either. If it weren't for me, if they'd heard the truth about our little interlude the other day, you would've been torn to shreds. Don't I get any credit for that?"

Belle's head was swimming. He was toying with her sanity and she was fast losing her resolve to ignore him.

"I told them you'd suffered a little fainting spell. That it was all a bit too much for you when I tried to kiss you and then it was lights out."

"You said what?"

"It's all right. They hardly focused on the fainting part. They were more interested in the fact that someone had tried to kiss Arabella Quinn. And that that someone was me." He laughed and Belle felt her stomach wrench into knots.

"But why?"

"I felt sorry for you," he replied. "I thought it would be interesting to create an air of mystery about you. To make the fools believe there's more to you than meets the eye. And you could do with some playmates. It can't be healthy spending all your time alone with a sketchbook."

Belle felt the heat of anger roiling within her. Compassion played no role in Noah's intentions, and she knew it. He was using her as part of some ridiculous charade.

"I don't need your help. Can't you see that there's no value in having friends like that. People who fawn all over you and be nice to you if it's dishonest? Or is that what you're used to? Haven't you ever had a real friend?"

"Have you?" Noah shot back and Belle narrowed her eyes.

"Perhaps not," she answered evenly, barely controlling her rage. "But at least what I do have in my life is honest."

"You know nothing about honesty, Redbella. I've caught you lying more than once. Trying to hide what you really think and feel, so don't pretend as though you're any better. I was doing you a favor. I would have thought you'd be more grateful."

"Grateful?" Belle almost shouted. "Are you serious? You humiliated me. You're playing stupid games and interfering in my life and you expect me to be grateful?"

A slow smile settled over Noah's lips as he gazed at Belle's flushed face. And she realized that once again, she had played right in to his hands.

"Calm down, red. It's all good. Only a bit of fun. There's no sense harping on about it. Besides…" he tapped his sketchbook with the pencil, "we don't have time for this. Didn't you say you wanted to get started?"

# Chapter Ten

Two weeks in to March, Belle sat with her sketchbook and pencil on her favorite branch of the Autumn Flame maple, admiring the way the golden leaves shimmered in the dappled sunlight. Some of them had begun to transform in luminous colors. She had already begun to fantasize about what she could do with the art competition prize money: contributing to Sidney's treatment, writing a nice check for her mother, securing a place to study fine arts at University being the obvious. The possibilities were endless. A light had appeared at the end of a long, gloomy tunnel and, though she knew it was foolish, Belle couldn't stop herself from dreaming of what could be.

There had been changes in the Quinn household. As Belle had hoped, Mum had begun to allow her to drop Sidney to and from school twice a week. It had given her mother some time to herself and she seemed a little happier, a little more relaxed than her usual frantic self.

And, of course, Belle was thrilled.

But Sidney had taken a turn for the worse. He was becoming fatigued on a daily basis, so much so that he was falling asleep in class almost every afternoon. Mum and Belle had taken him to see several doctors but none could find anything wrong. They suspected that at some stage, possibly when he had contracted Daisy's flu, he had suffered from glandular fever and was experiencing the after-effects.

Though Belle had not quite figured out how to deal with Noah, and she doubted that she ever really would, things had plateaued between them. His behavior hadn't changed, but she was learning to tolerate it. They had managed to do several drafts of their portraits and there were several months remaining in which to complete their final works, which relieved some of Belle's anxiety.

Anastasia, Brianna, Ben and Daniel still believed the lie Noah had told them and remained unnervingly civil to her. It had been alarming at first, but she found that she was getting used to it. It beat being pelted by basketballs and hiding in the bathrooms every lunchtime.

Belle's back was against a tree trunk as she leafed through the pages in her book and found her latest sketch of Noah. Something about it didn't seem right. She wondered if she was losing her touch, if maybe all the other times had been a fluke. Although the curves, lines and angles of the drawing captured Noah's features well enough, it seemed to lack something. There was something bland about it, something empty. She felt a stir in her stomach as she realized what it was. The drawing captured nothing but a shell, as though beyond the beautiful face and steely eyes, there was nothing inside.

# Chapter Eleven

The overhanging tree offered little shade, and though summer had officially passed, the afternoon sun was beginning to paint a pink flush over Belle's fair skin.

"Do you mind if we move?" she asked, eyeing Noah as he basked in the sunlight she sought to escape.

"Why? It's so nice here," Noah replied without opening his eyes.

Belle had anticipated such a response. "I know," she stated. "But I'm kind of starting to burn."

Noah opened one eye and ran it over her. Then he shut it again, clicking his tongue. "You should've worn sun block."

Belle gritted her teeth. "I am wearing it. But after a while it stops working."

"Then reapply."

Belle made an exasperated sound. "I don't have any with me."

Noah opened both eyes and rolled over, propping his chin in one hand. He leered up at her. "You could go to the office and get some."

Belle stared at him. He had already wasted twenty minutes of their time sun baking and now he expected her to go all the way to the office and back?

Noah laughed, looking as though he were enjoying himself. "Relax, we'll move. It'll be easier to see out of the glare, anyway."

They collected their things and made their way across the field, finding a patch of freshly mown lawn beneath three soaring eucalyptus trees. Belle sighed as she sat down on the cool, green grass and closed her eyes for a moment before attempting to persuade Noah to get to work. When she opened them, Noah was studying her, his face mere inches away.

"You're a little pink," he commented.

Belle rolled her eyes. "Well, I told you I was starting to burn."

"What do you look like under that uniform, anyway?"

"What?" Belle stammered, wondering whether she'd heard correctly.

"Under your clothes," Noah explained, as though it were a perfectly normal thing to ask. "Are you even whiter? Or are you all the same color?"

Belle couldn't think of how to respond and Noah chuckled, shifting closer to her. He took her wrist in his hand, tracing the tender, white flesh with his thumb. Belle shivered involuntarily and when she realized what she'd done, she glanced away in embarrassment.

"It's like your skin has never seen the sun," Noah murmured, his tone curious.

Belle pulled her wrist away. Noah had no sense of boundaries.

His gaze moved from her wrist to her face and he stared until she grew uncomfortable. "You're blushing," he noted.

"Yes." Belle exhaled, exasperated. "Thank you for pointing that out."

"Have I offended you?"

Belle felt her face grow even warmer under his scrutiny. She looked at her shoes. "No.. It's fine, really. It's all good."

But Noah wouldn't allow her to hide. He moved closer, humming a little as though trying to figure something out. "You're innocent, or something. Aren't you?" he asked in a low voice.

"I'm not sure it's possible for anyone to be truly innocent," Belle answered truthfully.

"Perhaps," Noah conceded. He tucked his arms behind his head as he stretched out on the grass. "But you misunderstand me. I meant that you're untouched."

Belle contemplated his words. If he was referring to what she thought he was, there was no denying it. So rather than incriminating herself, she kept her mouth shut.

"Tell me what you think of Anastasia," Noah said suddenly, changing the subject.

"Noah," Belle protested with a sigh. "I don't know her that well. I can't really comment."

"You're a smart one, red," Noah said in a low tone. "I've spent enough of my life liaising with society's best and brightest to know. And if my powers of analysis serve me well, I'd say you're not like most girls. Or most people, for that matter. So I want to know what you think. I want to pick your brain, unveil your insight. I want your opinion."

Belle shook her head, wondering what he was attempting this time. Surely he couldn't hold her opinion in such high regard, not when his values differed so greatly from hers.

"She's always been nasty to you, hasn't she?" he questioned, watching Belle's face intently. "Or at least she has been until recently. And now she's jealous of you. Jealous that something might be going on between you and I. That's why she's being so nice to you. Isn't it?" As Noah began to warm to his theme, his eyes brightened and a slow smile crept along his lips. "How does that make you feel? Does it make you feel good that someone who's always tormented you is jealous of you? That princess Anastasia might be questioning herself wondering if she's good enough? Wondering if there might be something you have that she's lacking?"

Belle wrung her hands in her lap as she chose her next words carefully. "I don't know if that's how she's feeling, Noah. But if you're right, it doesn't really change anything because it's based on something you told her, something that isn't true. So no, it doesn't make me feel good. I know I haven't really got anything that Anastasia could be jealous of."

Noah fell silent for a while. Then, to Belle's surprise, he leaned in and spoke in a husky voice. "Are you so sure of that? He pinned her with his piercing eyes and Belle's heart fluttered. "Are you sure that what I made them believe isn't true? Maybe you do have something that Anastasia doesn't have. Something she wants."

Belle was afraid to ask. But she found her lips forming the words before she had the chance to stop herself. "And what's that?' she whispered.

Noah smiled and leaned closer. He inhaled and she trembled, feeling as though he was smelling her as an animal might smell their prey. She felt a sense of danger that was as seductive as it was frightening.

"My interest."

Belle felt hot and cold and dizzy at once. As his breath lingered against her skin she knew suddenly and without any doubt that she had to get out of there. She stood abruptly and began brushing the grass from her dress. "Red?" she heard Noah's voice float after her as she collected her bag and began to walk away. Her knees felt weak and she stumbled a little. "Come on, I was teasing. I didn't mean it that way."

But Belle knew exactly how he had meant it, and it only made her legs move faster.

# Chapter Twelve

The lights came on and Belle flinched beneath the overpowering glare. She was trembling, her eyes trained to the thick, maroon curtains that hung before her, the lines she had carefully memorized already slipping from her mind.

The curtains opened and at first all she could see was blackness. But when her vision focused she was looking out in to a sea of faces, all of them with unblinking eyes that stared straight in to her. Her knees locked and her heart began whirring as she struggled to remember why she was there, what she was supposed to do and say. A cool breeze trailed across the back of her legs and Belle looked down to see that she was wearing only her nightdress, a thin, tattered scrap of material that barely reached her knees. And as she raised her eyes in horror she heard a murmur go through the crowd. Then the murmur became a chorus of laughter and suddenly she could make out the faces of Anastasia and Brianna in the front row, holding their sides, their eyes wet with tears of mirth.

Belle wished she could run, that her frozen body would comply with her commands. She closed her eyes and ordered her feet to move. But nothing happened. She was transfixed to the spot. And when her eyelids sprang open, her gaze became locked with a pair of ice blue eyes. They bore into her, glinting above a leisurely, condescending smile. Noah held up the script he was holding and tapped it with his finger.

"Well, red? What's the hold up? Everyone's waiting to see the show. Don't you realize it's all up to you?"

Belle started awake, bewildered and shivering. For a moment, the memory stayed with her, and then she saw her own room, felt the night breeze from the open window, and she released a shaky breath.

It had only been a dream.

\*\*\*

"Where are you going?" Noah asked as they sat near the tennis courts at the end of last period, sounding quite affronted at being deserted.

"Home," Belle sighed. "Like I do every Tuesday." Noah frowned at her as she packed her things and slung her bag over her shoulder. "Why do you run off every afternoon? I'm starting to get the feeling you don't like my company."

Belle rolled her eyes. "Not everything is about you,"

"Granted. But I was going to ask you something. I need you to do something for me."

Belle bit back a groan, wondering what he was going to request of her this time. It seemed that more and more she was playing the role of maid to Noah's every whim and she was getting tired of it.

"Do you think you could be my decision maker? You know, for important things."

"Excuse me?"

"My decision maker. I run something by you and you tell me what you think. Example: should I sleep with Anastasia at Ben's eighteenth next weekend? Yes or no. Simple as that. How does that sound?" He looked at her, a wide grin revealing his perfect teeth.

Belle blinked at him. He really was quite dazzling when he wanted to be. But what he was asking of her was ridiculous. She couldn't be expected to make that kind of decision for him. Belle sighed and shook her head. "I don't know. And I've got to go. I'm sorry. I'll see you tomorrow."

"Red," Noah caught her hand and pulled her toward him. "Stop for a minute. What's the rush? I want to know where you go every day. It's like you're Cinderella and you have to be home before the clock strikes midnight. Or three thirty in the afternoon, as I've gathered." He smiled at her and Belle wondered if there was any chance that he actually cared or whether he couldn't stand not knowing something.

Belle hesitated, glancing at her hand that was entwined with his. It looked tiny and white compared to his large, brown paw. Part of her was tempted to tell him about Sidney, yet a larger part knew it would be a fatal mistake. Noah Cole wasn't capable of sincerity. And she had already decided that Sidney was too precious, too important to her to allow Noah to know about him. If he ever wanted to hurt her, for any reason, he would only need to target her brother. And some things were sacred.

"My Mum's really strict," she said, choosing her words cautiously. "She doesn't like me hanging around after school. She likes to know I'm safe."

Noah had been tracing her palm in little circles with his thumb but he stopped, lifting his eyes to regard her intently. Belle hoped desperately that he wouldn't see through her feeble lie.

He dropped her hand unceremoniously and turned away. "Off you go then. You don't want to keep Mummy waiting."

Belle stared at him for a moment then shook her head in disbelief. She wasn't going to bite. Not this time. She wasn't.

So she straightened her shoulders, lifted her chin and walked away.

# Chapter Thirteen

"What's going on between you two then?' Susie asked, glaring at Belle from behind the thick rims of her glasses as they sat at the picnic table in the quadrangle. "You haven't told me anything lately. Are you doing it?"

"What?" Belle nearly choked on her sandwich. "Doing it? Are you kidding?"

"Kidding? Kidding?" Susie caught her glasses before they slid off the end of her nose. She adjusted them and peered at Belle scornfully. "I wish I were kidding. It's all I hear about in music every week for an hour and a half. *Do you think something's going on between Belle and Noah? Do you think I have a chance with Noah? Do you think I should ask Noah out? Do you think I should sleep with Noah?*" Susie made a gagging motion. "If I never hear Anastasia's voice again it will be too soon."

Belle dropped her sandwich into her lunchbox, her appetite vanishing. She cursed Noah under her breath for putting ideas in to everyone's heads. The seeds he had planted were growing and nobody but she was wise to the truth.

"So, I'm asking you to tell me. Is there something going on between you and Noah or not?"

Belle fixed her best friend with a frank stare. "I don't know what to tell you. There's nothing going on between us. I can't believe you even have to ask me that."

Susie eyed Belle shrewdly. "You're not a gargoyle or anything," she stated. "It's plausible that someone might find you attractive."

Belle ignored the backhanded compliment. "But Noah? When he's got Anastasia Asquith all over him? Come on. You don't really think that, do you?'

Susie looked doubtful. "I guess not," she said slowly. "But he's always touching you, and staring at you with this weird look on his face. Don't tell me you haven't noticed."

Belle looked at the ground. Of course she had noticed. It was impossible not to. Noah was constantly invading her personal space, breathing down her neck or staring her down with his steely eyes. But what Susie didn't know was that he had tricked Belle once with his strategic touches and whispered words and now she knew for a fact that he simply couldn't help himself. He was a notorious flirt and he took pleasure in making her squirm. And there was nothing more to it than that.

"He's just like that, Suze," she said with a shrug. "It's not only me he does it to. He's a player who puts the moves on any girl who's nearby. That's all it is. I swear."

Susie seemed to relax then. She smiled with the realization that Belle was still Belle who hadn't suddenly cranked her engine and overtaken her in the social world.

Susie and John had been growing closer during their art sessions and she would have hated the thought of her best friend landing a boyfriend before she did. Things were the same as they had ever been.

"Good," Susie said, sounding satisfied. "Because you know, as gorgeous as he is and all, he's bad news. I guess you were right. I mean, I feel sorry for him and everything, but where does he get off being so up in himself? I walked past him this morning and he didn't even answer when I said hello. It's not like it would have killed him. And if he's hooking up with girls like Anastasia then he can't be too smart."

Belle giggled despite herself. Susie had a point. And she only wished it were that simple, that Noah was nowhere near as smart as he thought he was. But Belle believed quite firmly in the unfortunate truth. That he was beyond clever.

He was too intelligent for his own good.

***

A week later Belle found herself once again studying Noah's face in the early morning sunshine. His smooth forehead creased as Belle attempted to get the correct angle on the thick, dark brows and angular forehead.

"Don't pull faces, Noah. Please, stay still. Your forehead's the hardest thing to get right."

"That's because I have the Cole brow," Noah declared with a flourish as he struck a pose.

Belle rolled her eyes, hiding a little smile despite her best efforts. "Did your father have it, too? Do you look like him?"

The grin died on Noah's lips and Belle had the feeling she had asked something too personal. "I'm sorry…" she began but he waved a hand at her dismissively.

"It's nothing. Forget it. Yes. Unfortunately, I look like my father. I always have."

"Unfortunately?" Belle asked surprised. "I would have thought…I mean, he must have been handsome," she finished lamely, feeling embarrassed as soon as the words were out of her mouth.

Noah laughed. "That's flattering, red. But the unfortunate part had little to do with his looks, believe me."

"Oh." Belle murmured, unable to think of anything else to say. Noah didn't elaborate, but after that, there was a heavy tension in the air that didn't quite seem to fade. She noticed that Noah's expression had changed, the arrogant rise of his chin replaced by something decidedly more vulnerable, and she couldn't help but wonder what his father might have done to inspire such resentment. They were silent as Belle put her head down and continued to work on her sketch.

"What about your family?" Noah's voice broke through the quiet a moment later. "You know, what's your story? Any skeletons in the closet? Scandals of note?"

Belle's eyes stayed trained to her drawing. "It's me, my brother and my mum," she said, hoping that would be enough to satisfy him.

"Hmm," Noah murmured thoughtfully. "No father?"

Belle shook her head. "He left when I was nearly six, eighteen months after my brother was born."

"He abandoned you, then. Why would he do that?"

Belle raised her eyes warily. "Well, I don't really know," she said honestly. Though she had always suspected that her father left because he couldn't deal with the burden of caring for a disabled child, but her mother had never confirmed the truth of that. In fact, Mum had never really spoken about it, ever.

Noah made a disapproving sound. "Sounds like a right prick to me."

Belle looked at him curiously. His audacity astounded her, yet she couldn't help but agree with him. It was unfortunate that Noah was as fascinating as he was infuriating. It meant that, if she wasn't careful, she ran the risk of being lured by curiosity.

"Please tell me he at least pays child support," Noah went on. "Though, from the looks of those shoes, I somehow doubt it."

Belle followed his gaze and realized he was staring at her scuffed, shabby school shoes she'd been wearing for three years straight. She frowned and stiffened. "No. He disappeared a couple of years after he moved out and we were never able to track him down. We've always kind of assumed he went back to Ireland."

"Ah. Ireland. Of course." Noah smirked as he ran a finger over one of Belle's crimson curls. "So do you have any other family out here? Anyone to help you out?"

"Well, his father, my grandfather, died before I was born. And *máthair Chríona*, who lived with us, died a year after my father disappeared. I never knew my maternal grandparents. They passed away when I was little. So no. We don't have any help."

"*Máthair Chríona*," Noah said thoughtfully. "Mother of the heart."

Belle looked up sharply. "How do you know that?"

Noah gave a smile that didn't reach his eyes. "Someone told me once, long ago..." He paused as though lost in thought. Then he cleared his throat and focused his gaze once more on Belle's face. "I'm sorry to hear about your family. And that you do not have help. It must be hard."

Belle looked at him, trying to gage whether he was being sincere. Unable to tell, she merely nodded. "I was a kid then, so I've forgotten a lot. But it is hard, sometimes. Yeah."

Noah bowed his head and for a moment he looked younger, his full mouth softened and his lashes glinting in the light. Belle took note, with the exception of that moment, Noah appeared older than most boys his age. She returned to her drawing and observed him in silence, recreating the piercing, long-lashed eyes, the curve of his petulant lower lip, the straight line of his nose and his hardened brow with her artist's hand. A few minutes later, she held her work away from her face and inhaled sharply as a little ripple of pleasure went through her. There it was. Proof that she wasn't losing her touch after all. And proof that there was more to Noah than met the eye.

"Let me see," Noah snatched the paper from her hand before she had time to stop him. She held her breath as he examined the drawing, his face remaining impassive as he scanned the page. And then his jaw tightened. "It's good," he said, flicking her a glance before his eyes returned to the paper. "Too good. I think I'm going to have to keep it."

Belle gasped. "No. You can't. I need it for my final work. This is the last draft before…"

"Too bad," Noah replied carelessly. "As I said, you can whip up another one in five minutes. This one's mine." He stared at her is if daring her to challenge him as he slid the portrait in to his sketchbook and tucked it in to his bag.

"Noah. Give it back."

Noah grinned smugly and raised an eyebrow. "Give what back?"

***

As Belle was eating lunch at the picnic table with Susie and John Cornwell later that day, an envelope dropped on to the table in front of her. Just as she was about to retrieve it, someone whispered in her ear, startling her.

"Ben asked me to give this to you," Noah's dark voice sent shivers down Belle's spine. "An invitation to his eighteenth. Do you think you'll be coming?"

Belle was too stunned to respond. She stared at the envelope, then at the equally stunned faces of John and Susie. Was Noah playing another prank? Her gaze slid toward him and he gave her a lazy smile.

"I… I don't think so," she stammered, trying to sidestep whatever trap he was setting. "Thank you. though."

"Come on, red," Noah slid himself in to the seat beside her and slung an arm around her shoulders. Ignoring John and Susie, he turned his intense gaze on Belle. "I can't go without my right hand man. You agreed to be my decision maker, remember?"

"Noah. I never agreed…"

"And I'm going to be making a pretty big decision that night if you catch my drift." Noah smiled slyly. He was so close that his breath whispered against Belle's face as he spoke. "So is it settled? I'll pick you up at seven thirty on Saturday?"

"Noah. I can't. My Mum… I…"

"You'll figure something out." Noah smiled winningly as he coiled a strand of her hair around his finger. "Please? Say you'll come."

Belle looked in to his bottomless eyes and grit her teeth. She knew that, one way or another he'd made sure she didn't have a choice. It was better to just give in. She lowered her eyes and nodded wearily. "Okay," she sighed.

"Awesome. Thanks, red. I'll catch you later." Noah let her hair slip from his fingers, stood abruptly and strode off.

Belle kept her head down, trying to delay the inevitable ear bashing that her best friend was about to dish out. Sure enough, after a beat, Susie cleared her throat.

"Well, I'm not sure about you, Belle, but it's pretty obvious to me what's going on here."

"Susie." Belle drew a deep breath. "There's nothing between us, I swear."

"Oh I can see that now," Susie said smugly. "No, something else is going on. I mean, you do realize what just happened, don't you? He said jump and you asked how high. You're in love with him, Belle. That's what's going on."

Belle's mouth fell open. Was Susie serious? Belle was not in love with Noah. Admittedly, she was not immune to his charms. He was a magnetic, intriguing person and she was human, after all. But loving him was quite another thing. It would be a form of suicide. The idea was ludicrous.

"Susie," Belle said stiffly, her lips tightening. "All I'm doing is trying to get through this year without making life more difficult than it has to be. And the best way to do that is to keep my mouth shut and go with the flow. When the year is over, I'll never have to see Noah again, and my life can go back to normal."

"If you say so, Belle," Susie replied with a meaningful look toward the nearby table where Noah and the popular kids were sitting. "But when this all goes pear shaped, don't say I didn't warn you."

Belle shook her head in disbelief, unable to think of anything clever to say in response. She eventually muttered an excuse about needing the bathroom, packed her lunchbox in to her bag and stood to leave.

"Walking away isn't going to change it," Susie called after Belle as she crossed the quadrangle. "You're playing with fire, Quinn. Can't you see that?"

# Chapter Fourteen

Belle had no idea what to wear to an eighteenth birthday party. She had never been to a party in her life and it struck her as odd that the first one she was going to was the birthday of a boy who, until recently, had been her arch enemy. She stared at her open wardrobe, willing one of her drab outfits to transform in to something sexy. For a moment she wished that Susie were there to help her.

Belle sighed heavily. All week, she hadn't been able to stop thinking about what Susie had said. She could hardly believe her friend had accused her of something that was so far from the truth. Belle had thought that Susie of all people would have understood the situation. She was the one who had wanted to be liked by the popular kids, who had dreamt of climbing the social ladder and making something of herself in the world of Pitts High. So why was she condemning Belle?

And then it clicked. Belle had been invited to Ben's eighteenth birthday party and Susie hadn't. Susie was jealous. Of course she was. It was what she had always dreamed of for herself. And if that were true, if she was indeed jealous, then maybe what she had said about Belle's feelings for Noah had been out of spite.

What if Susie had been wrong about Noah? Maybe he wasn't as bad as they thought. After all, he had tried to help her social situation, hadn't he? And her last sketch had captured a vulnerable quality she hadn't seen in him before. Maybe there was good in Noah after all. Sure, he was arrogant and shallow. Who wouldn't be when they had grown up with everything they could have ever wanted and more? And he was insufferable at times, moody, distant, and petulant. But he had suffered some terrible things in his life. Surely that counted for something.

Belle made a frustrated sound. She was never going to get anywhere thinking herself in circles. She needed to find an outfit within the hour or Noah would be there and she would have to go to the party in her dressing gown.

"Need any help, baby Belle?" Mum asked, sticking her head around Belle's bedroom door. She hadn't used that pet name since Belle was a little girl and it made her smile.

Belle noticed that her Mum was looking rather dressed up herself. Her dark, wavy hair was blown neatly and she was wearing a slimming black sundress and pearly beads around her neck. Belle found herself wondering if Mum might be excited about meeting Noah. She had granted Belle permission to attend the party without hesitation, which at first had struck her as suspicious. Belle hadn't questioned it but she soon considered the possibility that her mother might actually be happy that she was being more social, more normal like other kids her age.

"I don't have anything to wear." Belle gestured to her open wardrobe. "Everything I have is so…."

"Daggy?" Mum supplied dryly. She smiled at her daughter. "Ah, baby Belle. I wondered if this day was ever going to come."

"What do you mean?"

Mum looked at Belle and her eyes crinkled as she smiled. "You're growing up," she said wistfully. "My baby Belle is growing up."

"Mum." Belle blushed, glancing away. "Come on. Are you going to help me or not?"

"I think I might be able to," Mum said with a wink.

\*\*\*

Belle needn't have concerned herself about getting ready on time. Noah arrived over an hour late at nearly nine o'clock and didn't bother to come in and greet her mother. He honked the horn and waited for Belle to come to him.

"That's an interesting dress, red," he said as he turned the key in his brand new BMW Z8. The engine purred and the car slid forward effortlessly. It almost felt as though they were gliding.

Belle glanced out the window to see her Mum waving vigorously, her hair bouncing as she jumped up and down on the front porch of their tumbledown fibro house. Belle felt a rush of shame that Noah hadn't even had the courtesy to wave hello. She ducked her head and pretended she hadn't seen her.

"I like the green color, but it's a bit garish don't you think? Where did you find it, at the Op Shop?"

Belle grit her teeth as she looked down at the faux-satin dress her mother had given her. Apparently, Mum had been saving it for the year twelve formal as a surprise, having known that Belle would never have had the courage to go and buy an outfit. It was a lovely thought and Belle had been touched. She really didn't mind the dress, but, as much as she hated to admit it, Noah was right. It had been purchased second-hand at St Vincent de Paul's and it was rather garish. And it showed a lot of leg, which made her feel exposed and uncomfortable.

"Don't go all quiet on me. It was only a joke. You look fine. Forget I said anything."

Belle stared silently out the window, fiddling with the hem of her dress that was already starting to come loose. All the excitement she had felt at the thought of a night out was dissolving fast, and Susie's words of caution rang in her ears as they sped through the suburban streets. She wondered if she was making a huge mistake.

When they arrived, Noah opened the door for her and then collected a case of beer from the boot of the car.

"You're not eighteen yet," Belle pointed out as she set eyes on the case.

Noah looked amused as he lifted it on to his shoulder. "How did I know you'd say that? Shhh. It'll be our little secret."

As they walked through the front yard, Belle felt a flutter of anxiety in her stomach. There were people everywhere. Some were other students from school, some were older people who she assumed were Ben's relatives, and many she had never seen before.

Everyone was drinking. No one seemed to be without a bottle of some description. One couple was making out drunkenly by the pool while another nearby appeared to be arguing, the girl making aggressive arm gestures while the boy held up his hands in defense. Other people were dancing, talking and laughing loudly. Music blared from a large set of speakers that had been set up near the footpath and Belle had to cover her ears as they passed. A couple of boys from her math class were wrestling one another and one suddenly yelped and fell backward into the pool. Laughter broke out as water splashed everyone nearby.

Belle wanted to become small so that no one would notice her arrival. She hung back, hiding behind Noah as they reached the door.

"Hey shrinking violet." Noah glanced at her over his shoulder. "Can you carry these for me?" he handed her a couple of beer bottles. "I'm going to put the rest in the bathtub."

"In the bathtub?"

Noah grinned, pushing a lock of hair back from his forehead. "You've never been to a party before, have you?"

Belle was about to deny it when she resigned herself to how obvious her lie would be.

"It's okay," he leaned in and whispered in her ear. "Follow my lead."

Belle lagged behind as they entered the house and headed straight to the bathroom where, sure enough, the bathtub was filled to the brim with ice and various alcoholic drinks. Noah made some room and added several beers to the mix. When he was done, they made their way to the kitchen where a slim blonde woman in a skin-tight black skirt was fluttering about, preparing various hot and cold snacks and arranging them on platters.

"Can I give you a hand with that?" Noah asked smoothly, taking one of the trays from her grasp as she was lifting it.

The woman gave a little start and pressed a hand to her chest. When her eyes fell on Noah her expression changed and she began to smile widely. "How nice," she exclaimed and Belle was certain she saw her gaze skim over Noah's broad frame. "I've been going crazy with all this cooking. Of course Dave's no help as usual, always out back watching the bloody football." She rolled her eyes and pressed a hand once more to her ample cleavage. "Who might you be?"

"I'm Noah." He slid the tray in to his left hand while he held out his right. "I know Ben from school. And you are his sister I presume."

Belle almost groaned at his lack of subtlety, but the woman squealed and slapped at Noah's outstretched hand. "You cheeky boy. I'm Casey, Ben's mother, darl."

"His mother? Well, you must have had him very young."

Casey giggled and Belle cringed and looked away, unable to bear it any longer. When Noah was quite finished flirting with Ben's mother, he took Belle by the hand and led her out in to the backyard toward the raucous sounds of laughter and music.

"Ugh," Noah grimaced at Belle over his shoulder as he dropped the tray unceremoniously on to a nearby table. "Did you see that woman? Just when I thought people around here couldn't get any more common."

Belle was staring at him in amazement when someone grabbed her by the arm and pulled her in to a sweaty hug.

"Belle. You made it." Ben stepped back and grinned as he gave her the once-over. "Nice dress."

"Er, thanks," Belle smiled shyly, thinking that Ben seemed to be in unusually good spirits. "Happy birthday."

"Thanks, hun. Can I get you anything? Beer? Champagne? All you girls love champagne, doncha?"

"Uh…" Belle looked at Ben's face. His beady eyes were bleary and bloodshot. "No thanks. I'm fine for now."

"Well you owe me a shot later then, okay babe? Later." He pumped his fist in the air and staggered toward the outdoor table where Daniel and several other guys from school sat drinking and smoking cigarettes. He sat down and started laughing loudly at something then he lit a cigarette of his own and inhaled deeply.

Belle felt the nervous flutter spreading in her stomach. She glanced around but Noah was nowhere to be seen. She stood alone yet surrounded by people in the middle of Ben Carter's backyard. With no idea what to do or how she should act, Belle hovered and wrung her hands, scouring the yard for any sign of Noah. After a minute she spotted him. He was standing with one hand pressed against the veranda wall, leaning forward with his head bent slightly. Beneath his outstretched arm stood Anastasia, looking up at him through her lashes.

"Hey Belle. Nice dress." Brianna was suddenly blocking her view, standing so close that she could smell something sour on her breath. Belle jumped and took a step back and Brianna broke in to peals of laughter. She was wearing a tight, hot-pink tube dress that barely covered her chest or her bottom and the material rode up further as she laughed.

"Aww, look at you, all scared. I won't bite you. Unless you want me to." She winked suggestively. "Do you want a drink? I've got some passion pop if you're into that."

Belle glanced over Brianna's shoulder to where Noah and Anastasia had been standing but they had disappeared. "Thanks. I'm okay for now."

"Who are you looking for?" Brianna asked sweetly, looking in the same direction.

"No one," Belle said, forcing a smile. Brianna was eyeing her through her thick, heavily made-up eyelashes and Belle had the feeling that she knew more than she was letting on.

"Whatever you say, hun." She ran her hands through her sleek, dark hair and smiled. "Listen, I've got an idea. Come with me."

Before Belle could protest, she was being led by the hand and through the yard, toward the back door of the house. On the way, Brianna grabbed a bottle of passion pop and some plastic cups and tucked them under her arm.

Though she knew it was foolish, Belle couldn't help the little tingle she felt as they passed through the crowd. Everyone was staring admiringly and though she knew they were looking at Brianna and not her it made her feel good to be on the arm of someone who could command such attention. She felt attractive, worthy, like she mattered.

"Here," Brianna opened a door at the end of a hallway and behind it was another bathroom, minus a bathtub full of alcohol. Brianna pulled up a little stool and sat Belle down on it so that she was facing the mirror. Belle ducked her head to avoid looking at her own reflection.

"Stop that." Brianna pulled Belle's hair so that she was forced to raise her head.

"Ow," Belle yelped in surprise.

"Oh don't be such a wuss. As if that hurt." Brianna began rifling through her purse and pulling out various items. When she saw Belle looking at the impressive collection of makeup on the bathroom sink, Brianna explained, "I'm doing beauty therapy at TAFE."

"Oh. That's nice," Belle tried to smile but Brianna was yanking her hair back tightly and fastening it to the top of her head with a hideous tortoiseshell clip.

"We've got to get this stuff out of your face." Brianna stated, clicking her tongue. She unscrewed the top of the passion pop bottle, sloshed out two full glasses and began gulping at one.

Belle couldn't help but wonder where Noah and Anastasia had gone. Though it shouldn't have surprised her, she felt an undeniable flash of hurt at having been abandoned. They had come to the party together, after all. Didn't that count for anything?

"You know, your look might actually work," Brianna said thoughtfully, staring at Belle's reflection with her head tilted to the side. She took another sip from her cup and ran a hand through her hair. "The pale skin, the bright red hair. It's not my thing, but it could work. It could definitely work."

Brianna put down her drink and sat on the edge of the bath so that she was eye level with Belle. She ransacked her collection and selected some brown and grey shades of eye shadow, an eyeliner pencil, some shiny lip-gloss and some black mascara. "Close your eyes," she instructed and Belle did as she was told, sucking in a nervous breath. "Relax, ding, er, Belle. Keep your eyes closed and it'll be over in a sec."

Belle felt some gentle brush-strokes on her eyelids, the mascara brush combing through her lashes followed by a firm sweep of sticky gloss against her lips.

"Open," Brianna instructed and when Belle opened her eyes, it took a moment before she recognized herself. In the mirror was a girl who more closely resembled a model than Arabella Quinn. Her green eyes were made brighter by a frame of smoky shadow and black lashes, her lips were made fuller by the shine of the gloss and her face looked more structured, more defined by the sleek, swept back hair that was piled in scarlet coils on top of her head.

"Not bad, huh?" Brianna's tone held a note of self-satisfaction as she slid the makeup collection off the bench and in to her handbag in one sweep. Several items clattered to the floor but she didn't seem to notice. "I think that calls for another drink."

But Belle couldn't take her eyes off herself. She leaned closer, wondering if the girl in the mirror really was her. Upon closer inspection, she could see that the eye shadow was a little uneven and there was a glob of mascara in the corner of her left eye but the effect was still mesmerizing. Belle had never seen herself look so pretty.

"Come on, I want to show off my skills to the rest of the crew." Brianna stood up and took Belle by the hand. "Stop staring at yourself and get up."

Before she could think, Belle was being dragged out of the bathroom and into the hallway. It was dark and narrow and Belle stumbled as Brianna collided with something and came to an abrupt halt.

"Ow," Brianna yelped. She flicked on a light switch and suddenly they were under a bright, fluorescent glare. Belle blinked and it was a moment before her eyes adjusted. And there, straight in front of her, Anastasia and Noah were entwined against the wall, her arms around his neck, his hands at her waist and their lips only inches apart.

# Chapter Fifteen

Belle felt as though she'd been punched in the stomach. The blood drained from her face and her legs become unsteady. "Ew. Guys, can you get a room?" she heard Brianna say, but everything suddenly sounded like white noise in her ears. "Come on, Belle, let's get out of here."

As they walked past, Belle caught Noah's eye and the coldness in them sent a shiver down her spine. She thought she heard Anastasia whisper, "Thanks for taking care of her," and Brianna replied in a hushed voice, "No worries."

And then it all became excruciatingly clear.

Outside, the air had become crisp and Belle relished the breeze as it cooled her flushed face. She felt an unpleasant tingling, as though adrenalin was pumping through her veins, and she breathed deeply, trying to stay calm, trying not to allow her emotions to creep up to the surface.

"You okay, babe?" Brianna asked chirpily, collecting two more plastic cups and filling them with passion pop. She stretched herself out on the back steps next to Belle. Belle had chosen a quiet spot, a dark spot far from the rest of the rowdy party guests. "I think you might need some of this." Brianna held the cup under Belle's nose and swirled it. It smelled of passion fruit and cider and something a little sour. Nowhere near as awful as Belle would have imagined.

"No thanks," Belle said, but there was less conviction in her voice than before and Brianna picked up on it at once.

"Come on," she urged. "Look, I'm sorry about Noah. I know you guys had something going for a while, but it's nothing personal. Anna really likes him. And she always gets what she wants. There are plenty of other guys out there. Anyway, this will make you feel better. I promise."

Belle eyed the cup warily. It didn't seem so bad. It smelled okay. And God knew she did want to feel better than she did at that moment. Why shouldn't she try it? Belle took the cup in her hands and lifted it to her lips.

"Here's trouble," a familiar voice said from behind her and Belle jumped, spilling some of the passion pop in to her lap. Noah chuckled as he sat down beside her. "This is new," he said with a bemused twitch of his lips, eyeing her face and the plastic cup pointedly.

"I gave her a makeover." Brianna bragged. "Doesn't she look hot?"

Noah ignored the question, keeping his eyes trained on Belle's face. She burned under his scrutiny, wishing she could disappear, that he would go away and leave her alone. "You don't scrub up too badly, red. The shadow's a little heavy but it brings out the green in your eyes."

Belle turned her head but Noah wouldn't allow her to escape that easily. "You're not really going to drink that, are you?" he whispered against her ear. "You've got nothing to prove, you know." Belle jerked away from him and he clicked his tongue. "Don't be mad with me, red. I need your help. I need you to make a decision for me."

By that stage, Brianna had lost interest and wandered off to join her friends. She staggered a little in her heels and two guys stood up to help her across the treacherous, pitted pavement. Noah took the opportunity to slide his arm around Belle's shoulders and pulled her against him.

"Where's Anastasia?" Belle asked, astounded by the accusation in her voice.

"Waiting for me," Noah said lazily, smiling his slow smile. "In the bedroom."

Belle turned to him. He actually expected her to decide whether or not he should sleep with Anastasia? Was he out of his mind?

"It's your call. What's the verdict?"

Belle shook her head in disbelief. "This is a sick game, Noah. I won't play it."

"Whatever do you mean?" he asked with a lift of his eyebrows, stretching his arms over his head as though he didn't have a care in the world.

"You know exactly what I mean. This stupid game, whatever it is, I don't want any part of it anymore. Please, stop."

"So you're saying that you won't decide for me?"

"No, I won't."

"Well, in that case I suppose I have no choice." He gazed at her through sleepy lids, the expression in his eyes unreadable. "I'm going to have to sleep with her."

"No," Belle shouted before she could stop herself. She clapped a hand over her mouth but it was too late. Noah fixed her with a piercing stare and smiled slowly.

Belle's stomach sank as she was struck by her own unwitting confession. She lowered her head in defeat, trying to hide her shame as it burned within her. "I was wrong, Noah," she whispered. "I had thought there was some good in you. But I was wrong."

At that moment, Noah clasped her wrists and drew her close to him. He pressed his mouth against her ear and whispered harshly, "Don't be mistaken, Belle. This is, and always has been, nothing more than a social experiment. Don't you see that it doesn't matter how it turns out? Haven't I made you understand by now? The problem with you, is that you think there is good in people when there isn't. You want to believe in something that doesn't exist. You want to see me mend the error of my ways. But this is me. I don't want to be any different. It is only you who wishes me to be something more than what I am."

When he released her wrists, Belle was trembling. "But you could be, Noah," she said, her voice wavering with hurt and indignation. "You have been given so much and yet you do nothing good with it. You toy with people, hurting instead of helping them. You play cruel, horrible games. You never serve anyone but yourself."

"Given so much? All that ever mattered in my life has been taken away. You know nothing of what I have been forced to go through." Noah's eyes were fierce as he glared at her. He glanced around then leaned in, lowering his voice. "And when you claim that I haven't exerted myself, well, I seem to recall exerting myself on your behalf to save you from almost certain social death."

"You did that for your own amusement." Belle whispered hoarsely, her voice hitching in her throat. "After you played the prank on me to begin with. You said it yourself. This is nothing more than an experiment to you."

"Well, maybe it was at first."

"What do you mean *at first*? You just said…"

Noah threw his hands up. "Haven't I left Anastasia waiting while I sit here talking nonsense with you? Haven't I decided not to sleep with her at your command? Don't I listen to your word above all others?"

"I don't… I don't understand."

Noah's jaw tightened and his face became closed. His eyes were cast in shadow as he regarded her. "And it's best if you don't." He stood slowly and ran a hand over his face. Then he sighed and held out his hand.

"Tick, tock, Cinderella. It's almost midnight. Time to take you home."

# Chapter Sixteen

Sidney was coughing noisily when Belle entered the kitchen on Monday afternoon and she frowned with concern. Mum shot her a disapproving look as she bustled past, holding up her watch to show that it read half past three.

"Sorry Mum," Belle sighed, throwing her bag on to the kitchen bench. "You still have that cough, Sid?"

Sidney shrugged. "I guesso. Iss not that bad, Beyya."

"Yeah, but you've had it for a while now. How are you feeling? Are you still tired? Did you fall asleep today?"

Sidney rolled his eyes. "No. Well, only fo a lil bit."

"Aw Sid... is that every day this week?" Belle bit her lip. Crap. She sounded like her mother. "Don't worry about it. I'm sure you didn't miss much. Here, I'll make you some chocolate milk. That'll perk you up."

Sidney's eyes lit up, but then, his lips drooped and he frowned. "I'm fine, Beyya. I don wan you to worry. I already make Mum worry. 'Sides, Mum said I cahn haff chocolate milk today."

Belle shot him a sly grin as she spooned two heaped tablespoons of powedered chocolate in to a mug. "Well, Mum's not here, is she?"

Sidney grinned back and Belle noticed then that he was looking a little pale. His cheeks seemed more prominent than usual and she wondered if he was eating enough. She plonked the chocolate milk in front of him and instructed him to drink up. Then she collected his laptop and homework and began setting it up.

"Beauty and the Beast, huh?" she commented as she pulled a copy of the children's fairytale from Sidney's bag. "How come you guys are studying a kids' book?"

Sidney swallowed a gulp, most of it dribbling down his chin, and shrugged his shoulders. "Not really a kids' book. Iss actually really cool. Iss the real one, not Disney or anything. Iss about this shallow guy who turns away an old woman who needs help juss because she's ugly. Then she turns in to a beautiful woman and casts a spell on him to make him ugly so he knows what it feels like. The spell can only be broken if someone falls in love with him even though he's a beast. Tha moral of the story is about loving someone fo wass on tha inside, I guess. Even if the ousside's a wit wonky. Like you do fo me."

Belle glared at Sidney as he grinned at her through his milk moustache. "Don't talk about my brother that way," she warned, wiping the milk from his face. "That's a load of crap. You're beautiful."

"Only 'coz you see me that way, Beyya. And some day someone's gonna see you that way too." Belle tried to smile but it came out as more of a grimace. Sidney tilted his head and looked at her with concern. "Sorry Beyya. I didden mean…"

Belle shook her head, waving a hand at him. "Don't worry, Sid. I know you didn't mean it like that. I guess I'm tired too."

"Beyya." There was a warning note in her brother's tone. "Yo not telling me sumthing. Woss wong?"

Belle felt her eyes sting a little at his kindness, that he had the heart to worry about her trivial problems. But when she looked in to his gentle, brown eyes, she felt the sudden urge to divulge everything, to unburden herself from the confusion and angst she'd been drowning in.

"His name is Noah," she confided, her voice barely louder than a whisper. She thought she saw a flicker of understanding cross her brother's face and she ducked her head in embarrassment.

"Who's Noah?"

Belle stared at the table in front of her for a moment, contemplating that question. Who was Noah? And why did she care so much for an arrogant, self-centered boy she barely even knew, and what she did know was bad?

"You know what, Sid?" Belle said with a weary sigh. "He's the guy from your story."

When Sidney didn't reply, she looked up and noticed that his eyes had drooped and he had fallen sideways at an awkward angle in his wheelchair. One arm was twisted beneath him and the other was twitching as it rested against the arm of the chair.

Belle's blood ran cold. "Sid," she yelled, standing so fast her stool clattered to the floor. She was at his side in an instant, checking his breathing, his pulse, his pupils, going through all the motions she had been taught in her first aide course. All the while, her heart was hammering wildly in her chest, icy panic creeping over her at the possibility that something might be terribly wrong. Once she established that he was breathing and his heart was beating she grabbed the phone and called an ambulance.

\*\*\*

"You did the right thing," the paramedic, whose name was Jim, said to Belle, smiling kindly at her as he strapped Sidney in to the stretcher. "And I don't want you to worry too much. We're only going to take him in to run some tests to make sure he's all right. But, as you know, seizures are common with this kind of cerebral palsy."

Belle nodded, unable to take her eyes off her brother's pale face as they began to wheel him through the kitchen.

"Has he had seizures before?"

Belle nodded. "Only once or twice. And only when he's really tired. He hasn't had one for years. We thought maybe he was lucky and grew out of them."

Jim nodded. "Yes, some are lucky and do grow out of it. But seizures are unpredictable, as you know. Looks like he might've had a relapse. Has he been unwell lately?"

"The doctors think he might have had glandular fever a while ago. So yeah, he's been really rundown."

"Right. Well, that's probably the trigger then. Not to worry, we'll take care of him tonight and have him back as good as new in the morning."

Belle tried to smile, but her mouth wouldn't cooperate. She watched with a heavy heart as they lifted Sidney in to the back of the ambulance and then she climbed in beside him.

\*\*\*

Belle slept in Mum's bed that night, as she had done after a bad dream when she was a little girl. They had wanted to stay at the hospital with Sid, but the doctors persuaded them that, seeing as it was nothing critical, the best thing they could do was get a good night's rest and come in early to be there when he woke up.

All night, Belle stared at the ceiling, unable to fall asleep. She kept envisioning Sidney's pale face as he was lifted in to the ambulance. She kept agonizing over the guilt of not having paid better attention to him, of having been complaining about something so trivial when it happened.

And the negative thoughts didn't stop there. She began cursing the injustice of it all, how cruel it was that beautiful little Sidney had been afflicted by such a heartless disease when there were less deserving people in the world who had everything and took it for granted.

Life is unfair, she thought bitterly as she slipped in to a fitful sleep, finding comfort only in the fact that she was not the first to think so.

# Chapter Seventeen

"The time has come," Mr. Whitworth said with an air of finality, glancing around the room at each of the students. "There will be no more class time allocated to work on your portraits as of today. As you know, your visual arts major work is due in October, so most of your class time from now until the end of the year will be dedicated to that. From her on, you are going to need to find time out of school to finish your final portraits. Your task today is to make a regular date with your partner, one you can both stick to, in order to get those final works more or less finished by the due date."

Belle felt an unpleasant heaviness settle over her. Aside from the prospect of spending even more time with Noah, the drama with Sidney had started to take its toll and she was beginning to fall behind in her schoolwork. Though Belle usually got good grades, she often wondered how she managed to do so as she rarely spent much time studying. Despite her other duties, it was usually a result of forgetfulness or her preoccupation with sketching, but this time she had a proper reason and it was starting to worry her that she might not be able to get everything done in time.

"Don't forget," Mr Whitworth continued, ignoring the groans that filled the room. "It's a part of the assignment that you get to know each other. So you have five minutes to plan where and when you're going to meet. And I want it to be some time this week. Off you go."

"So," Noah drawled, sauntering up to Belle's table and leaning across it, "your place or mine?"

Belle looked down, trying desperately to think of a reason why they shouldn't go to her place. Besides not wanting Noah to know about Sidney, there was the equally alarming possibility that he would spend the entire time mocking the squalor in which she lived.

"Yours," she answered quickly, gnawing on her lower lip. "If you don't mind. Our place is being, uh… renovated at the moment. Everything's in shambles, there wouldn't be any room."

Noah eyed her shrewdly, as though he knew exactly what she was trying to do. He looked for a moment as though he might protest. But then he stood up and shrugged carelessly. "As you wish. I live in Fairside, so it's a drive. About half an hour or so. You can follow me there after school on Friday."

Belle dropped her eyes. "I don't have a car."

"Oh." Noah fixed her with an unreadable stare. "Can't you borrow your mother's?"

Belle bit her lip, knowing she'd be pushing it to spend a Friday away from Sidney as it was. Though Mum had been more reasonable of late, Belle couldn't ask to borrow the car on top of expecting her mother to hire a babysitter.

"I can try."

Noah waved a hand dismissively. "Don't bother. You can come with me and I'll drop you home. No big deal."

Belle's jaw dropped a little. "Thank you," she said in astonishment.

***

Belle sucked in a nervous breath as several students, including Anastasia, Brianna and Daniel, began milling around the parking lot to watch them drive off. If she hadn't been so anxious she might have laughed at Anastasia's stormy expression.

"Princess Anastasia hasn't been speaking to me since I left her high and dry," Noah commented with a twist of his lips.

"Can you blame her?" Belle retorted coolly.

Noah didn't respond, but she thought she saw him hide a smile. "How come you don't have a car?" he asked as they turned on to the winding country road that led to the coast. Belle wondered whether he was tormenting her again or whether he genuinely had no idea that some people couldn't afford to buy their seventeen-year-old children brand new BMWs.

"We can't afford more than one car," she answered, hoping he wouldn't ask any follow up questions.

Noah made a disapproving sound. "You need a car," he said gruffly. "It's freedom. You're trapped without one."

Belle agreed. She wanted to remind him that some people didn't have the luxury of a choice.

"Your family's really that poor, then?" he asked needlessly. "Tough break."

"We're not poor." She hated that word. It didn't to do justice to her family's situation.

"Oh? And what are you then?" Noah queried, and she wondered if it was amusement she detected in his tone.

"We may not have a lot of money," Belle replied softly, "but we're not squatting in a ditch somewhere. Or pawning jewelry to get by. We're not bogans."

Noah's loud and sudden laughter startled her. "So growing up in the boon docks doesn't qualify you as a bogan? Well, that is interesting. You really do learn something new every day." He continued to chuckle as Belle's cheeks burned. She stared out the window, watching the trees and houses go by, promising herself that she would learn to keep her mouth shut.

Fifteen minutes later the countryside began to change and the ocean came in to sight in the distance. They reached the top of a steep crest and began to descend in to a leafy little town on the shore of a velvet blue ocean. The scenery was beautiful and Belle found herself breathing deeply of the crisp, sea air.

"We're close," Noah said as they passed a well to do looking school with a high wrought-iron fence lining its vast perimeter. "Fairlight Grammar School" the sign at the front declared.

"If you hate Pitts so much," Belle began, "then why do you go to school there? I mean, couldn't you just go to that school?"

Noah kept his eyes fixed directly ahead. It was a moment before he answered. "I spent many a holiday in Fairside growing up. I know people around here. I chose to attend Pitts because I wanted to remain inconspicuous. If it were up to me, I wouldn't be going to school at all." And with that, he fell silent once more.

Belle supposed it was natural to want to avoid running in to people who had known his family. It would be excruciating to have to endure their pity and answer those prying questions. Once again she felt the tug of sympathy as she glanced at Noah's solemn profile.

When they reached the bottom of the hill, the ocean was before them, stretching out as far as the eye could see. Majestic yachts and cruisers lined the shore and when Belle looked to her left she didn't need to imagine to whom they belonged. The houses on the hillside were impossibly grand, some of them two and three stories high with vast balconies, rooftop swimming pools and plush, manicured gardens.

"Here we are," Noah said as they pulled in to a steep driveway that rose beneath a looming, four story mansion. Belle pulled in a sharp breath. The house was almost obscenely large. Taking up nearly two blocks, the immense, layered structure was an imposing presence on the hillside, dwarfing the surrounding houses with its tall pillars and seemingly endless rows of arched windows. It was more a castle than a house.

Noah parked in the driveway and got out, but Belle sat for a moment in awe. It was hard to imagine living in such a place. How did they keep it so immaculate? They had to have a lot of staff.

Noah appeared at her window and opened her door. "Are you going to get out or just sit there gaping?" he asked with a smirk. Belle flushed and scurried out.

They made their way up a flight of wide steps to the front door and Noah led her through into what appeared to be a foyer. A winding staircase rose from its center and disappeared in to the high ceiling. Surrounding the stairs were four arched doorways that, she presumed, led to various rooms. "Through here. We'll work in the living room, there's better lighting," he directed and Belle followed him through the foyer and into one of rooms to the right.

Despite herself, she gasped when they entered. The living room was as large as a house. Certainly as large as hers. Shelves were adorned with fine objects, awards and various trinkets that stretched toward an impossibly high ceiling. Beautiful artwork and family portraits in gilded frames hung on the walls, and vast windows lined with golden drapes revealed a stunning ocean view. Something about the room resembled photographs Belle had seen of the Italian wing at the Louvre museum – a place she had always longed to visit. She glanced up, half expecting a replica of Michaelangelo's famous ceiling from the Sistine chapel.

"This is amazing." Belle exclaimed, unable to contain herself. She placed her bag on the sleek wooden table that faced the enormous windows and walked around the room. "It's... wow. I don't have any words for what this is." She walked in a slow circle, taking in everything. How did he live in such a place every day and ever get anything done?

Belle paused when she realized Noah wasn't speaking. She turned to him and saw that he was staring at her. "What?"

Noah's expression was impenetrable as he pushed a golden lock from his forehead. "You're so easily impressed. Most of the girls I've had here..." he trailed off and didn't say anything more.

Belle couldn't help but wonder what kind of girl wouldn't be overwhelmed by such decadence. She tried not to imagine how many girls he'd had there. This wasn't a fairy tale castle and Noah was no prince. Just because she was in his house and it had been a while between insults didn't change anything.

"Let's get started then," she said quickly, recovering from her momentary insanity. "Mum's only given me two afternoons and then our only choice is early mornings."

Noah stepped forward and was suddenly right beside her. He took her by the shoulders and turned her so that she was facing the wall with her left side to the window.

"Stand there," he ordered, using a finger to reach around her body and tilt her chin up. He was standing so close that she could feel his breath in her hair.

Belle frowned and was annoyed that he was, once again, invading her personal space. It seemed a strange position to put her in and then Belle saw where he had placed his drawing material on the table. "It's not supposed to be a profile portrait," she protested.

"Who says?"

Belle's shoulders sagged. She was never going to win an argument with Noah.

"The project outline didn't specify that the portraits have to be front on."

"But aren't portraits usually - "

"You have a nice profile. I think it will turn out better this way."

"Fine." Belle's heart began to thud a little faster. He had paid her a compliment. She felt his hands brush her arms and the cool breeze from the window whisper across her neck as he pulled her hair back, lifting it away from her skin. Belle sucked in a breath and held it.

Her heart started hammering as she felt a finger trace the back of her neck.

"As I thought," she heard him mutter. "Clammy."

She released the breath she had been holding and turned to see Noah shaking with laughter.

"You can't help yourself, can you?" she muttered. She didn't want to play his games anymore. She wanted to get her work done and get out of there. A glance at the grandfather clock in the corner of the room told her it was nearly half past four. "Can we please get started? It's getting late."

Noah didn't seem to hear her. "You know, if you cut your hair, or wore it up like you did, you wouldn't get so hot. It must be like having a rug on your head." He chuckled and reached forward to lift a tendril of hair away from her face. Belle flinched. "It's okay, I won't bite. Just think about. You might have more potential than you think."

Noah let the tendril fall back against Belle's cheek and went to take a seat at the table. He took up his sketchbook and a graphite pencil and made a little twirling motion with the pencil in the air, indicating for her to turn around.

Grudgingly, Belle grit her teeth and did as he commanded, turning to face the wall and tilting her chin up slightly.

"Perfect," he declared and her shoulders sagged with relief.

It had to have been thirty minutes later when he said, "Almost done." Belle stretched her aching muscles. Every time she moved, Noah had snapped at her and she had stood so rigidly her neck and shoulders hurt. As she stared out the window she saw that it had started to rain.

Noah was adding the finishing touches as a loud bang echoed from the foyer, making Belle jump and Noah's eyes widen.

"Who could that be?" Noah muttered, but before he could finish his sentence, a figure appeared in the doorway, startling both of them. A tall, elegant woman stood holding a briefcase and an umbrella, a tailored suit fitted neatly around her tall, slender frame and her greying blonde hair pulled back tightly in a stylish French twist.

"I'm not interrupting anything, am I?" the woman asked, her fine eyebrows arching with cool amusement. Thunder sounded from the distance and the room was cast in shadow as clouds began to gather in the sky.

Belle glanced from the woman to Noah, hoping that somebody would explain what was going on.

"Aunt Bethany," Noah said darkly and there was no mistaking the contempt in his voice.

# Chapter Eighteen

"Be a dear and find somewhere to put this," Noah's aunt addressed him in an accent similar to his as she waved the sopping umbrella in the air. "It started bucketing down the moment I stepped out of the car. I would have parked in the garage but someone's vehicle was blocking both entrances."

Noah's jaw clenched visibly as he stood to take the umbrella and deposited it in a large urn that sat near the doorway. "I wasn't expecting you. Why didn't you use one of the garages out back?"

"It wouldn't do to come in through the back door. I could have given you quite a scare."

"You already have," Noah muttered and Belle slid him a curious glance.

Aunt Bethany didn't seem to notice. She embraced Noah and pressed a swift kiss to his cheek. "My boy. How are you? How are you coping? And who is this… this delightful creature?" She smiled widely at Belle but her eyes remained untouched by emotion. Belle noticed that they were the same ice blue as Noah's.

"I'm doing as well as can be expected," Noah answered smoothly. He gestured to Belle. "This is Arabella Quinn from school. We're working on an assignment together."

"How nice. Is that what they're calling it these days?" Aunt Bethany chuckled, glancing at Belle with a raised eyebrow.

Belle plucked up her courage. "It's nice to meet you," she said as politely as she could, resisting the sudden compulsion to curtsey.

"Likewise," Aunt Bethany returned with a flash of pearly teeth.

"What are you doing here?" Noah said coldly, clearly in no mood to play host to his aunt. "Don't you have places to be? Souls to harvest?"

"Noah," his aunt snapped, losing her poise momentarily. She recovered herself, smoothing a hand over her perfectly groomed hair. "There's no need for that kind of talk. You know why I'm here. To see my favorite nephew, of course."

Noah's eyes darkened. "You've wasted your time. What you're looking for is not here."

Aunt Bethany eyed her nephew coolly. "We'll see," was all she said.

With her head swirling, Belle looked from Noah to his aunt and back again, awaiting a cue as to what to do next. Lightening flashed, illuminating the room for a split second and then returning it to near darkness.

"I should go," she began uncertainly, inching toward her bag that rested on the table. "Is that okay?"

"No," Noah barked, startling her. She looked at him in surprise. "You should stay, Belle. It's going to storm and it won't be safe to drive until it clears. You can use my phone to call your mother." He reached in to his pocket and pulled out his mobile. He tossed it to her and she managed to catch it between both hands.

"Thanks," she whispered.

"Splendid." Aunt Bethany exclaimed, her voice ringing with false cheer. "There'll be three of us tonight then. Noah and I will give you some privacy, dear, while we see what to do about dinner. I don't suppose Esther has come with you, Noah? I do miss her famous canard al orange."

"No," Noah replied, slanting Belle a glance as he followed his aunt out of the room. He switched on a lamp, casting a warm, amber glow upon Belle's face. "I am quite alone."

Belle stared at the phone in her hand then at the empty doorway in shock. She couldn't figure out what had happened. Why had Aunt Bethany shown up unannounced? Why had Noah treated her so coldly? And why was he so desperate for Belle to stay? There was something unnerving going on in this house and she was completely at a loss as to what it might be.

With a sigh, she began to fiddle with the phone, trying to figure out how to make it work. Once she'd managed to unlock the screen she keyed in the number for Pitts Hospital and waited for it to ring. She got through to the front desk and was transferred to the appropriate ward.

"Hello?" her mother answered almost immediately, sounding short of breath.

"Mum. It's Belle."

"Belle. Is something wrong? Are you with Sidney?"

Belle sighed. "Not yet. I'm sorry. I'm still at Noah's. It's starting to storm here and Noah thinks it's best if we wait until it passes. His aunt is here and she's invited me to stay for dinner."

The silence rang in her ears as she awaited her mother's response. "Well. I suppose that's reasonable. As long as his aunt's there I guess there's no harm. I'm sure Rebecca won't mind staying until I get back."

Belle exhaled with relief. "Thanks, Mum. I'll let you know when I'll be coming back. It shouldn't be any later than nine."

"Be safe. And Belle?"

"Yeah?"

Belle wasn't sure, but she thought she heard a little chuckle. "Have fun."

***

The family portrait hanging in the center of the far wall had only three people in it, a man, a woman and a little boy. The picture was undoubtedly Noah and his parents. The blue eyes and golden curls were unmistakable. But there was a light in his eyes that Belle had not observed in the Noah she knew. His mother had been tall and slender, like Aunt Bethany, with vivid green eyes and a cascade of glossy brown hair. Noah favored his father, who was blond and blue-eyed. The mother wore diamond earrings and a pearl necklace, and the father wore an unusual, golden ring on his left pinkie. The collet of the ring formed the shape of a pentagon, and at its solid gold center, a simple V symbol was embossed. Belle was stepping forward to inspect it more closely when Noah's voice startled her.

"Did you reach your mother?"

"Yeah," Belle replied, embarrassed at being caught off guard. She handed the phone back to Noah. "Thank you. She says it's fine to stay for dinner. I was looking at your family portrait?"

"Yes. They are my parents," Noah replied in a neutral tone.

"You look like your father," Belle said, trying to alleviate the sudden tension. Noah frowned and nodded and she wondered if her comment displeased him. "And your mother... well, she's stunning."

"She was the most beautiful woman in the world," Noah agreed and Belle was surprised to hear such warmth in his voice. "A woman of true class and grace. Something you would never understand." He glanced at Belle with a little smirk but she ignored him, deciding she could let that one slide.

"She was from England, you know. She became a successful model. Felicia Faye was her name before she married. When she moved to Australia she worked in PR mainly with some high profile clients. That's how she met my father. She was the total package.. If she hadn't got sick, she could have ruled the world. That's what she wanted. That's the kind of woman she was. And that's the kind of woman she'd want me to be with."

Belle nodded, unsure if there was anything she should say in response to that. It was understandable that his mother would have wanted her son to find someone she considered worthy of him. Every mother wanted that for her child.

"She made me promise," he continued, almost as though he were talking to himself, "when she was dying, she made me promise. I often sat at her bedside and watched the cancer eat her away. One night she made me vow that I would marry someone she would approve of. Someone with class, grace, and good breeding. She didn't want me to end up like…" he trailed off and cleared his throat abruptly. "So that's what I'm doing. That's what she would have wanted. You understand, don't you?"

Belle wasn't sure she understood any of what had transpired at the house that afternoon and yet she found herself nodding slowly. It seemed as though he was asking for approval of what he had shared.

"I know what you're thinking." ·

Belle looked at Noah in confusion. He was behaving strangely, even for him. "What do you mean?"

"You're wondering why I promised my mother I would find a woman of class and social standing and then go about with girls who are… well…" He shrugged and his eyes twinkled a little as he smirked. "Beneath me, if you will. But you have to understand, I don't plan to marry any of those girls. When choosing a wife, breeding is the only thing that matters. She needs to be educated, intelligent and sophisticated. She needs to be able to handle herself with dignity in exclusive social circles. She needs to be capable of producing an heir worthy of my family's legacy. Anyone who comes before that is only practice." He chuckled. but there was something odd about the sound.

Belle felt a little stab at the finality of his statement. So there was no hope, not in a million years, of being anything more to Noah Cole than a lower class acquaintance. She was not surprised. She hadn't expected any different. But that did little to take the sting from the truth.

"I'm here until the first of June, my eighteenth birthday. God knows what my mother would have thought of me being at Pitts High of all places. The idea would have turned her stomach. But I know she would have understood, given the circumstances. Her will signifies that as soon as I turn eighteen I get it all. I inherit my parent's fortune and am given full power of attorney. I am the sole heir, you see. Bethany never married or had children and my father's brother died when they were boys. I decide who gets what, and when, if anything. That's the only reason I came here. To wait it out. To get away from everyone who..." He stopped short, looking at Belle sharply. He shook his head. "I have no idea why I'm telling you this. Anyway, that's the situation. Soon I'll be out of your hair and you can resume your ordinary little life."

Belle had the unsettling feeling that after all of this, after her partnership with Noah was brought to an end, she might never be able to go back to her ordinary life. Her heart sank a little as it hit her that their days together were numbered.

"I've called every restaurant in town and nobody will drive out in this wretched weather," Aunt Bethany declared mournfully as she entered the room. "Is there anything in that infernal kitchen that's actually edible?"

Noah looked mildly amused as he regarded his flustered aunt. "Neither Aunt Beth nor I have any idea how to cook." He said secretively, seeming to find it entertaining. "It's a symptom of being revoltingly spoiled, I'm afraid."

"I know how," Belle said before she had time to stop herself. Two pairs of ice blue eyes turned and pinned her in an instant. Noah ran a hand through his tousled mane and gave a slow, lazy smile.

"Off you go then, red."

# Chapter Nineteen

"Wherever did you *find* this girl?" Aunt Bethany addressed Noah in a shrill voice. "You'd never know it to look at her, but she's quite an exceptional chef. Rather a step up from your usual…" she trailed off, slanting a sly glance at Noah. "Well, never mind that."

If Noah was bothered by his aunt's snide remarks, he didn't show it. As the three of them sat at the enormous dining room table, Noah had committed himself to devouring his meal in under five minutes. "This is really not half bad. I'm not a fan of risotto, but I'm making an exception in this case."

Belle found herself flushing with pleasure. She wasn't good at much, but with a mother who worked nights and a dependent brother, she had learned to cook from a young age. And she had rather enjoyed cooking in such an amazing kitchen. It had everything she could have ever needed, and all at arm's length. She had felt like she was cooking in the kitchen of Buckingham palace for the Queen. And it was clear that Noah had not been exaggerating about his family's lack of culinary skills. Belle had found plenty of things in the fridge and cupboards to use.

"You shouldn't allow him to speak to you that way," Aunt Bethany told Belle.

"It's all right." She shrugged and gave a little smile.

"Well, what nonsense, I won't hear of it. Particularly after you have made us such a fine meal. Apologize, Noah."

He almost choked on a mouthful of risotto. He swallowed carefully and slanted Bethany a dark look. "Tread carefully, Auntie dearest. You're lucky I've welcomed you into this house as it is."

"The house isn't yours yet, my boy," Bethany articulated clearly, a glint in her frosty eyes. "And until that day comes, I believe that I could ask you to leave."

There was silence as aunt and nephew stared each other down. Belle looked at her plate, wishing there was something she could do to ease the tension. And then a clap of thunder sounded from above and everyone jumped in their seats. The booming noise had shaken the mansion to its foundation. Bethany fluttered a hand at her chest and Noah put down his fork and set his eyes on Belle.

"I think you should stay the night."

Belle had been reaching for her glass of water and her hand froze in mid air. "What?"

"I know it's not ideal, but look." Noah gestured to the windows behind him as a flash of lightening lit up the sky. Belle could see that the rain was pelting down as heavily as ever. They were so sheltered on the ground floor of the mansion that she had thought that perhaps the rain had stopped.

"I'll call your mother, if you like," Aunt Bethany offered.

Belle gazed out at the stormy, black sky and sighed. There didn't seem to be any alternative.

***

Belle laid in the huge, soft bed, surrounded by pillows and covered by a light, cotton blanket. The room smelled of lavender and cinnamon from the perfumed sticks that sat in a vase on the vanity. The heavy velvet drapes masked most of the light from the lightening flashes that flickered across the sky.

On the fourth floor, where all the bedrooms were situated, the sound of the rain was much louder as it struck the roof above her head. Belle felt out of place in the massive space, dwarfed by the looming bookshelves and eclectic array of objects, no doubt collected on various overseas trips. Their shadows cast by the amber light of the lamp that stood by the doorway were a bit eerie. She found herself longing for her cozy, little bed at home with its mismatched sheets and familiar smell.

A quarter to twelve and Belle could not fall asleep. Every time she thought she might be drifting off a clap of thunder brought her awake with a jolt, and she was back to square one. To make matters worse, there was a strange scuffling noise that seemed to be coming from the hallway every few minutes. It made her anxious, causing her to imagine that it might have been an intruder or, though she didn't believe in such things, a ghost.

As she was beginning to drift off again she heard a rattling sound coming from behind the door. Belle's eyes snapped open and she sat up in time to see the doorknob turn and the door open slightly. Belle clasped her hands to her throat as her heart leapt.

Noah's golden head appeared around the door, his eyes seeming luminous in the low, amber light.

"Are you awake?"

Belle couldn't find her voice. Her heart was racing with fright and she wasn't sure whether she should be relieved that it was Noah or more terrified. She nodded mutely.

"Good. Can I come in?"

Belle hesitated, suddenly aware that she was barely covered by the thin cotton shirt she wore under her uniform. But something about Noah's eyes compelled her to let him in. She pulled the blanket up to her neck and gave a nod and Noah slipped inside, shutting the door behind him.

"Thanks," he said in a hushed voice, stealing silently across the room. He was wearing a pair of pyjama bottoms and nothing else. Belle lowered her eyes, trying not to look at his bare chest. Noah reached the bed and sat on its end. For a startling moment Belle thought that he looked almost frightened.

"Is something wrong?"

"Yes," Noah said, pinning her with his stare. "I want to ask you something."

Belle blinked, wondering what could be so important that he had decided to sneak into her room so late at night.

"Can you do something for me." He paused and crouched forward, taking both her hands in his. His touch was warm, almost hot. "Can you do something for me, Belle?"

She stared at their hands entwined on the bed and couldn't help but wonder if it was another trick. He had asked so much of her already and she wasn't sure there was anything left to give.

"I'm not sure."

"I know I don't deserve it. I know I've been a right prick to you and I can admit that. But I need help, Belle. And you're the only one I can trust."

His words had such an effect on her that she began to tremble. How dare he do this? How dare he say to her that he needed her, knowing full well that she could never refuse him? She was about to pull her hands away when he tightened his grip.

"Please, Arabella?"

Perhaps it was the way he said her name or the anxious glint in his eyes as he looked at her. Perhaps it was that she was exhausted and had no strength to argue, or that being in his house, having him sitting on her bed and holding her hands was the straw that broke the camel's back.

"What do you need?" she asked him on a sigh.

Noah's face relaxed. He brought her hands to his lips and kissed them soundly. Then he reached hurriedly in to the pocket of his boxers and withdrew something. He took her hand in his and pressed a small, hard object against her palm.

Belle slowly raised her hand and inspected what he had handed her. It was a ring. A heavy, golden ring with a pentagonal collet and a V symbol embossed at its solid gold center. It was the ring Belle had seen Noah's father wearing in the portrait.

She raised her eyes to Noah, a thousand questions swirling through her mind.

"Can you keep a secret?" he whispered, his steely eyes looking almost fierce as they searched hers. "If I tell you something, can you swear you'll never tell a soul?"

She looked down at the ring and traced it lightly with her index finger. It was beautiful. And strange. She had no idea what he was asking of her, yet she found herself saying, "Yes."

"Swear it."

"I swear."

Noah sighed and closed his eyes briefly. Then he started to speak in a low voice, and Belle had the feeling that he was sharing something he had kept inside for a long time.

"This is… was my father's ring. Only ten were created, and he was given one. My father was a member of an exclusive association for Nobel Peace Prize winners. They had all achieved something of greatness, contributing in a profound way to the improvement of humanity. My father received his prize for his philanthropic work during the September eleven attacks and for his dedication to reporting the truth and depicting both sides equally. Few journalists had dared do such a thing, especially about that day. Shortly afterward he was given his ring and initiated in to the group. They called themselves the Altruist Society. V is the symbol of peace and the pentagon represents balance and completeness. Equality."

Noah was watching Belle closely as if to gage her response and she nodded to show that she understood.

"This ring is extremely valuable. Not only because it is made of solid gold, but because of what it symbolizes. It opens many doors. The bearer is permitted entry to any exclusive event in the world. Political, social, charitable, even royal. You name it. So you can imagine my aunt's obsession with it. Why she is so keen to get it in to her conniving clutches."

Belle's eyes widened. Who would have thought that such a small object could wield such power? She had never heard of anything that came close to what Noah had described. But she believed it. It was within the realm of imagination that someone would want to possess such power. Though it was not something she had ever yearned for, she knew there were many who did.

"It is a key to the world, in many ways. Aunt Bethany claims my mother intended to leave it to her. That she was planning to change the will at the final moment but that she died before she could. A load of rubbish. My mother would never want her wretched, jealous sister to inherit the ring. Neither of my parents would want to see it fall in to the wrong hands."

Noah clenched his fists and Belle saw a muscle twitch in his jaw. He leaned closer, lowering his voice to barely a whisper. "Bethany is contesting the will. She has hired a team of lawyers to go over it with a fine-tooth comb and find any microscopic flaw, any technicality that will permit her to snare this from under my nose. The first of June can't come quick enough."

Belle exhaled slowly, gazing with fascination at the ring as she turned it over in her fingers. It gleamed, reflecting brightly in the low light. "I understand why it is so important," she said carefully, "And why you don't want anyone else to have it. But it was your father's. And I thought you didn't… I mean, the way you talk about him."

"He was a hypocrite," Noah said bluntly. "He didn't deserve the prestige and the accolades he received. He didn't deserve the ring. But that doesn't mean I'm going to let Aunt Bethany get her hands on it."

Belle nodded, wondering once more what Austin Cole could have done to arouse such hatred in his son. But did Noah think that *he* deserved the ring and everything it represented? Or was it merely a case of not wanting it to fall in to the wrong hands?

"Keep it for me. Please, Belle. Keep it for me and guard it with your life. I can't wear it, God knows. I don't feel it would be right. Besides, Bethany wouldn't think twice of searching me in my sleep."

"But won't your aunt suspect that I have it? What if she comes looking for it?"

Noah shook his head. "No. She knows I would never part with it. That I would never entrust it to anyone. She wouldn't think to search you."

Belle looked at Noah in awe. If what he was saying was true, then why was he entrusting it to her? What if she damaged it, or worse, lost it? Belle squeezed the precious ring tightly in her fist, thrilled and terrified at once.

"It's safe with me," she vowed, meaning it, and before she knew what was happening, Noah clasped her face in both his hands and kissed her firmly on the lips.

"Thank you, Belle. Sweet Belle." He traced her cheek softly with his finger as she sat in stunned silence. His eyes were warmer than she'd ever seen them and his gaze lowered to her lips and lingered there for a moment. Belle held her breath.

But Noah pulled away, raking both hands through his tousled hair and squeezing his eyes shut. "It's really late," he murmured, dropping his hands, not meeting her eyes. "I should go. You should sleep."

Belle nodded, not trusting herself to speak. Surely she was dreaming. Surely this strange night was a figment of her imagination and she had hallucinated their entire conversation.

"Do you have somewhere safe to keep that?" Noah asked, glancing at Belle's tightened fist. Before she could answer, he went to the vanity, opened a drawer and pulled something out, something that glinted in the amber light.

"Here." He revealed a length of gold chain, took the ring from Belle's clasp and threaded it on to the necklace. "It was my mother's." He fastened it around Belle's neck and tucked it securely beneath her shirt as she watched in silence. Her hands went to her throat when he was finished and she traced the fine gold chain with her fingers. It felt cool and smooth against her skin. Yet her cheeks were hot. She couldn't help wondering how much he could see through her flimsy t-shirt.

"No one will ever look there." Noah smirked, his eyes resting on her face for a moment. He smiled slowly and Belle thought she saw a glimmer of the familiar Noah, the one she knew. "Goodnight, Belle. Sweet dreams."

# Chapter Twenty

Belle did not have sweet dreams that night. After a fitful sleep, she woke the next day wondering if the events of the evening had all been her imagination. And then she felt certain that it had been all in her imagination because when Noah greeted her in the morning it was as though nothing had changed, as though nothing out of the ordinary had happened the night before. The only reminder was the heavy, golden ring hanging around her neck.

When, at long last, Belle arrived home, it felt as though she had been away for weeks. She flopped onto her bed and stretched out her limbs, sighing luxuriously. She was exhausted after a night of interrupted sleep and felt like she could lie there for a thousand years.

And then she felt the weight of the ring against her chest and her hand went to the neck of her school dress. She pulled gently on the chain and the ring emerged, gleaming in the light as it had the night before. Belle turned it over, a feeling of warmth filling her at the knowledge that Noah had trusted her with something so precious. She closed her eyes, remembering the feel of his lips on hers. They had been soft and warm, yet firm. It seemed he was asking something of her without taking it, which was strange when they both knew that, against her better judgment, she would not refuse him.

She turned her gaze to the window and saw two flame red leaves snatched from their branch by the wind. They twirled and tarried through the sky, looking like two dancers entwined in a waltz, before floating to the ground.

By the time all the leaves had fallen from the tree, Noah would be gone.

\*\*\*

Susie didn't acknowledge Belle when she sat down beside her in math. She stared straight ahead, pretending she hadn't seen her.

Crap. It was going to be one of those weeks. Sidney had suffered another, mild seizure and had been prescribed anticonvulsants, which he had to take on a daily basis. Mum was more flustered than usual with the added worry, and Susie hadn't spoken to Belle much since she had gone to Ben Carter's party with Noah.

Belle had spent her lunch hour making awkward conversation with Brianna and her hangers-on and she found herself missing the familiarity of Susie's company. Her only comfort was the weight of Noah's father's ring against her skin, a constant reminder of the secret they shared.

Miss West, the math teacher, had her back turned as she scrawled a quadratic equation on the board and Belle took the opportunity to tap Susie on the arm. Susie slid her a cursory glance and Belle smiled tentatively. "How've you been?" Susie raised her eyebrows and shrugged. "How are things with John?" Belle had noticed that John and Susie had been spending more time together and were looking pretty cozy.

"What do you care?" Susie whispered.

"I care," Belle replied. "So are you two going out?"

Susie looked as though she might ignore the question but then a telltale smile crept across her lips. "Maybe. Yeah. I think so."

"That's great." Belle said excitedly and as she leaned over, the golden ring rolled out from beneath her uniform and dangled in the air between them. With sudden panic, she snatched it up and tucked it back under her dress, but not before her friend's sharp eyes honed in on it.

"What's that?" Susie hissed, reaching forward at once. Belle clapped her hands over her chest and Susie shot her a strange look. "It looked like a guy's ring. Why won't you let me see?"

Belle's mind went in to overdrive as she tried to think of an excuse for why she would be wearing a ring around her neck. But as the seconds ticked by and Susie's eyes began to narrow, Belle decided to tell the truth. "I'm sorry, Suze, but I can't. It's kind of a secret and I promised I wouldn't tell."

"A secret? Who with? Who'd ask you to keep a...." Susie trailed off and her lips curled in a sneer. "Right. It figures. Noah."

"No." Belle hissed, darting her eyes to the front of the room, but Miss West hadn't seemed to notice their exchange. "No, it's not him. Really. It's not."

Susie rolled her eyes then turned to Belle and glared at her. "I know you're lying, Quinn. It's so obvious. You've changed, you know. It's like I don't even know you anymore. Please don't pretend like you care what's going on with me when you won't even tell me what's going on with you."

And though Belle made several attempts to talk to Susie again, that was the last thing she said.

# Chapter Twenty-One

"Is Aunt Bethany still here?" Belle asked warily as she entered the foyer. Noah's aunt's presence had been tolerable once, however, after finding out about her devious plan, Belle didn't particularly fancy another encounter.

Noah laughed. "She stayed for three days and tore the place apart. Naturally, she didn't find a damn thing. I'm sure she'll focus her energy on horsewhipping her team of lawyers from now on. All I can do is pray they come up with naught before June." He placed his things on the living room table and stood by the window, looking out at the grey mist that rose above the ocean. "I know my mother. The documents will be airtight. I don't think I have much to worry about now. Thanks to you."

Belle smiled self-consciously as Noah glanced at her over his shoulder. His expression was almost warm and, though it should have pleased her, she found it unsettling. He had been treating her with civility more and more of late and she kept waiting for the punch line, but it never came.

"Do you want this back, then?" Belle asked uncertainly, fingering the delicate chain that rested against her throat.

Noah took a step toward her and replaced her fingers with his. He lifted the chain and cast an appraising eye over the ring. "You've kept it safe so far," he said in a low voice, his fingers brushing her throat as he turned it over in his hand. "And you never know what Aunt Bethany has planned. It might be best for you to hang on to it for a while."

Belle couldn't deny the sweep of pleasure she felt at his words. Had he asked her to give it up, it would have felt as though they were severing the fragile bond they had forged, that what little good she had managed to find in her partnership with Noah would be lost. She couldn't hide the small smile that stole across her lips.

"You don't smile often," Noah commented and Belle blushed. "You should do it more. I like it."

There he went again, being nice to her. Belle searched for an appropriate response, wishing for the thousandth time that she had been blessed with wit and confidence. Thankfully, a resounding bang interrupted the silence, echoing loudly through the room and causing them both to flinch. They looked up to see that a gust of wind had blown closed the paneled windows that faced the ocean.

"You must be bad luck," Noah muttered, crossing the room and fastening the bolts on the windows. "Every time you come here, it starts to gale."

A short while later, Noah was growing restless. "Why is it taking forever?" he complained, fixing Belle with a petulant glare. "What happened to whipping up one of your little sketches in five minutes?"

Belle lifted an eyebrow. "I seem to remember having to stand still for much longer than fifteen minutes," she replied. "But I guess we can take a break. My hand's kind of getting sore." Belle flicked her wrist to relieve the tension.

"Awesome," Noah stretched his arms over his head and sighed. "What do you want to do? Are you hungry? After you were here last time I went shopping. I figured I may as well be equipped for the occasional guest."

Belle stared at him for a moment before smiling. "Yeah. That'd be great."

Noah left to get the snacks from the kitchen and Belle occupied herself with a tour of the mansion. The last time she was there she had only glimpsed a fraction of it and she was curious to see the other rooms. She wandered through the arched doorway, into the foyer and through another arched doorway. The room appeared to be a display room of some kind with trophies and medals filling the shelves that lined its perimeter. More enormous portraits in gilded frames hung on all four walls, the subjects looking like ghosts inhabiting an abandoned castle.

Belle took a turn around the room, admiring the items on display. She couldn't locate the Nobel Peace Prize, but it occurred to her that it was probably kept in the family's Sydney home. Disappointed, she contented herself with perusing the other items on display. She noticed on one of the shelves that a small, framed picture seemed to have been pushed back, hidden behind an unusual wooden carving of a mythical, horned beast. The frame protruded from one side of the statue and Belle stepped forward and pinched the corner between her fingers. She withdrew the frame carefully and blew the dust from the glass panel in the front.

The same golden haired little boy, older than he had been in the portrait in the living room, and the same man and woman, smiled back at her. Young Noah's stiff smile was sandwiched between waves of perfectly gelled hair and a neat little bowtie. He didn't look at all happy, and his disgruntled expression made Belle smile.

His parents were as beautiful and as immaculately dressed as they had been in the first portrait. But there was another person in the picture, a young woman with wild, strawberry-blonde hair and bright hazel eyes who didn't appear to resemble anyone else. It seemed that she was standing a little behind the others, as if to separate herself from them somehow. The girl was pretty, in a natural, un-groomed sort of way, but she appeared terribly plain beside the imposing good looks of the Coles.

"Snooping around?" Noah asked as he entered the room carrying a tray. He set it down on a low, mahogany coffee table and poured a glass of lemonade and a beer. "Don't you know that's rude?"

Belle quickly placed the photo on the shelf and dropped her hands. "This place is so amazing," she confessed, gesturing around her with both hands. "I couldn't help it. I have no idea how you live in all this space. Don't you get…" she stopped abruptly, realizing what she had been about to say.

Noah's eyes seemed to glow in the dimming light as he approached her. He pursed his lips as he handed her the glass of lemonade. "Lonely? No. I've spent most of my life alone. In fact, I prefer it that way."

Belle smiled, surprised to find that they actually had something in common. "Me too," she said softly. "I suppose maybe I thought… I mean, I might get scared in such a big place. A little. Maybe." She felt self-conscious and turned her head toward the picture she had been looking at. She cleared her throat. "Who's the woman in that photo? I haven't seen her before. She's not in any of the other portraits."

Noah followed her gaze and when his fell on the photograph his lips tightened. Belle wished she could say at least one thing right.

"Sorry. Is she your sister?" Oh God, she thought. What if he'd had a sister and she had died too?

Noah shrugged as he took a sip from his glass. He placed it on a coaster and took a step toward the picture in question. "You may as well know. She wasn't my sister. Her name was Alice and she was our au pair. She was from Ireland, originally."

"Oh." Belle said in surprise as she thought of her own *máthair Chríona*. She fingered a lock of her hair, noticing that Alice's was a shade of red as well, though much lighter.

"She came to live with us when I was about nine. She was a lot of fun, right from the start. Everybody loved her. Everybody," Noah's voice was bitter and it didn't seem to match his words.

"But you didn't?" Belle asked softly.

"Oh, I loved her too." Noah laughed yet the sound was forced. " I had a bit of a crush on her, actually."

Belle was taken aback. Though Alice seemed pretty enough, she wasn't the type she thought Noah would go for.

"Yes, it's true. I had a fondness for the lovely Alice back in the day. And, unfortunately, so did my father."

Belle had been raising her glass to her lips as Noah spoke, but her hand froze in mid-air. Noah chuckled darkly when he saw her face. "Surely you heard about that? It was all over the papers. Though perhaps you were too young."

Belle's surveyed Noah's solemn face. Was he kidding? Had his father really had an affair with the nanny?

"Don't look so alarmed. It happens. The short version of it is they had an affair and he was planning to leave my mother for her. Primarily, I suspect, because she was carrying his illegitimate child."

Belle's fingers flew to her lips. And as she stared, something clicked. Noah's father had betrayed the family, had betrayed Noah. And then he had died. No wonder Noah's feelings toward his dad were so emotionally charged.

"It was leaked to the media," Noah continued, that strange, distant quality returning to his voice. "I am still unsure how it got out. But the result was devastating. The paparazzi went wild. They stalked my father, my mother, me. They didn't let us have a moment's peace. My father was ruined. He had been hailed as a hero, an upstanding family man, and something of a modern day saint. And he crashed and burned. It was brutal, really. Six months in to the relentless pursuit of his demise, he committed suicide. After that, amazingly enough, the media left us alone."

Belle felt as though something cold, like a bucket of ice, had been thrown over her. Her skin tingled as it sank in. Noah's father had killed himself. After everything he had done to the family, after everything they had already endured. Belle felt tears spring to her eyes.

"Noah." She stepped toward him, reaching out her hands. "I'm so sorry."

"Don't be," he snapped, stepping back abruptly. "I knew you'd be this way. I shouldn't have told you."

"No," Belle whispered, startled by his sudden transition. "I'm glad you did. I'm sorry. I didn't mean…"

"I said don't be sorry," he repeated, waving away her outstretched hand. "They got what they deserved. He died and she and that little brat are living in a pauper's paradise, in the slums of western Sydney. My mother made sure of that. She made sure they never got a penny of my father's money, which I suspect is what Alice was after all along. That's what they get for destroying my family. That's what they deserve."

Belle stared at Noah as his lips twisted in a strange, malicious smile. She shivered, her hands still at her lips, torn between pity for Noah and his family, and horror that his father's young mistress and an innocent child had been punished so cruelly for what had happened.

For a long time, neither spoke. But soon Belle's instincts got the better of her and she took a tentative step forward. "Noah I didn't know. Thank you for telling me. I'm sor… what I mean is, I feel for you."

"Spare me," Noah said, his lips curled in a sneer. "As I said, karma has taken care of it for me. And I will take care of the rest. I will make sure no one inherits what is rightfully mine, what remains of my family's legacy. Not Aunt Bethany, not that slut and her bastard child. No one."

Belle flinched as Noah's voice echoed in the vast space. By then the sun had set and the room was shrouded in near-darkness. Belle wrapped her arms around herself, noticing the chill in the air.

"Do you want me to go?" she whispered, her voice sounding small in the enormous room.

"Go?" Noah responded, looking surprised. And then his expression changed as his eyes flashed. "So that's it, then? You get me to confess it all, to tell you my secrets, and then you leave? Did you finally find what you were looking for and discover you didn't want it after all?"

"What? No. I thought, if you wanted me to…" "Well, go then. I don't need anyone's pity, least of all yours. Go on. Get out of here. Go, he yelled."

Belle froze for a moment, paralyzed by the force of his command. Then she turned, her hands shaking, and began to walk away. As she was about to clear the archway, she heard an anguished sound and turned to see Noah clutching fists of his hair. She stopped and stared at him in horror.

"Don't leave. Please. Don't leave me," Noah stepped came forward and gathered Belle to him, pressing kisses to her face, her cheek, her throat. And though she meant to pull away, she didn't. She wound her fingers in his hair and parted her lips beneath his.

He kissed her feverishly, clutching her, his hands gripping her waist. She felt the full length of his body against her and was thrilled by it. Suddenly, he wrenched away, panting, and then he pressed his mouth close to her ear.

"Don't leave me. Swear it," he pleaded, his breath like fire on her skin. Belle felt his tears, hot and wet, falling against her cheek, trickling down her throat as he choked against them.

"Noah," she whispered in disbelief, her arms reaching around him. She held him to her chest as he sobbed brokenly, soaking the front of her dress. "It's okay, it's all aright," she crooned, kissing his cheek, sliding her fingers through his hair.

"Promise me," he whispered, raising his head to look at her. His eyes were glistening and bright, tearing at her heart. They were beautiful, even then. Especially then.

"I promise."

# Chapter Twenty-Two

The light was blinding as Belle's eyes flickered open and she found herself facing an open window. Sunlight streamed through the parted curtains, casting a warm glow on her face, but something was amiss. Her surroundings were unfamiliar, even the mocha-colored sheets were unfamiliar, and she sat up with a start when it dawned on her where she was.

She was in Noah's room.

Belle's hands flew to her chest and her fingers brushed the familiar, textured cloth of her school uniform. She looked down and sighed with relief. She was fully clothed. The events of the previous evening began to trickle into her consciousness. It had stormed. Again. She had called her mother. She and Noah had talked long in to the night, had held each other and kissed and...

Heat flooded Belle's cheeks. Noah had kissed her. She had kissed him back. The way he smelled, the way he felt was all coming back. She had felt things she'd only dreamed of, had been introduced to a world of sensation, desperate and thrilling. And they had fallen asleep in each other's arms. But what did it all mean? And where was he?

Belle took a deep breath and waited until her heart stopped whirring. Then she threw back the covers and stood up on shaky legs.

"Running out on me?" a voice came from her left and Belle's eyes darted to the doorway to see Noah standing in nothing but a pair of boxers, leaning against the doorframe. She felt her cheeks redden and quickly reached down to tug on the hem of her dress.

"Sorry," Noah frowned, running his eyes over her crumpled uniform. "I should have found you something to sleep in."

"It's okay," Belle waved a hand at him. "I'm fine."

"Would you like something to eat? Drink? I can make instant coffee and, well, that's about it." Noah smiled then looked at his feet. Was it her imagination or did he seem nervous?

Belle shook her head. Impossible. Her heart beat faster and her fingers twitched at her sides. What was he thinking? Did he regret what had happened? Did it change anything? How was she supposed to act?

Noah's gaze lifted to rest on her face and he smiled. "It's okay, Belle. Your virtue remains intact. The dress, and everything else for that matter, never came off. I kept my hands to myself all night. I promise. And you needn't worry, I won't tell anyone about this if you don't."

Belle looked at Noah and felt a knot of pain pull within her. She understood his meaning perfectly. And as she observed his smooth, composed face, so different from last night, she felt the knot tighten.

She ached to push the hair back from his face, to see that raw, honest look in his eyes once more, to hold him and never let go. She didn't want to hide it. She wanted the world to know. But she was no fool. She had never dared to believe that she could be anything more to Noah than this. The previous night had been the result of suppressed grief, of desperation, and nothing deeper. That he could feel the same as she did was impossible.

With a deep breath, Belle tucked her emotions firmly away and forced a smile. "Don't worry. It'll be our secret."

*** 

The carpet of blood red leaves crunched beneath her feet as she slipped through the gate and into the backyard. There was no time to dwell on what might have been. Her weekend was jam-packed. She had a ton of study to catch up on before an early start at the pharmacy the following morning and she was babysitting Sidney tonight night while her mother had dinner with her rarely-seen girlfriends. It was not lost on Belle that her mum had more of a social life than she did.

Sidney was looking tired as he sat in his chair, a sandwich sitting untouched in front of him.

"You okay, little bro?" Belle asked, depositing her bag on the bench. When he heard her voice, Sid looked up and grinned.

"Howwas it?"

"Fine," Belle shrugged, ducking her head a little and hoping he wouldn't ask any follow up questions.

"You're back late," Mum commented as she crossed the living room with a basket of laundry under her arm. She raised her eyebrows pointedly as she began pegging the wet clothes on the indoor clothesline. "It's not like you to sleep in."

Belle nodded, avoiding eye contact with her mother. "We had a late breakfast and did some more work this morning." She gritted her teeth, hating the lie even as it came out of her mouth.

"How's his aunt? Did she feed you well? I'll bet that family dines like royalty." There was a note of something in Mum's voice that Belle couldn't quite decipher.

"Ah, actually we ordered a pizza. Nothing special," Belle said, leaving out the part that Aunt Bethany hadn't been there.

Mum seemed to brighten. "Oh. Okay then. I guess the rich eat take-away too sometimes."

Belle smiled in understanding. On an impulse, she crossed the room and put her arms around her mother. "Love you, Mum," she said, a lump forming in her throat. For some reason, she craved a hug from her mother more than anything at that moment.

Mum stiffened for a moment then put an arm around her daughter and patted her awkwardly. Belle felt her sigh. "Well, I love you too baby Belle. You know that, don't you? Now go on with you. The day's half gone and I don't want you stressing that you're falling behind."

"Yes, Mum." Belle sighed and reluctantly let go.

***

"Belle. Belle. *Arabella Quinn.*" Mr. Whitworth was dashing across the playground, waving a small slip of paper in the air.

At the sight of him, Belle got to her feet and went to see what was the matter. By the time they met half way across the oval, Mr. Whitworth was out of breath.

"Belle, I'm so sorry. I'm the bearer of bad news," he puffed, glancing down at the slip of paper he held then handing it to her. "I have a message. Your mother rang. It's your brother. He's been taken to hospital."

Belle tensed, a jolt of adrenalin running through her. Sid was in hospital. Again. He had another seizure, or worse. How was she going to get there without the car?

Mr. Whitworth touched her hand and smiled kindly. "It's all right, my dear. I'll drive you. Come on, let's go."

***

The fluorescent lights were beginning to hurt Belle's head as she dashed down the seemingly endless corridor, her eyes peeled for room 108. She spotted the number at the end of the hallway and ran to it, reaching the doorway at last and practically skidding through it.

"Slow down before you hurt someone," Mum said in a hushed voice. She beckoned for Belle to come closer. Belle tiptoed across the tiled floor while taking in her brother lying unconscious on top of the crisp, white sheets of the hospital bed. His little face was pale with dark circles rimming his eyes and he had a tube coming out of his mouth. A strange contraption that resembled an accordion stood next to the bed, emitting a strange, robotic, breathing sound as it stretched out and then contracted again. Belle knew there hadn't been one of those the last time Sidney had come to hospital.

"What's that?" Belle asked. "Is he all right? What happened? What's wrong with him?"

Mum sighed, looking drawn and grey as she ran both hands over her face. "He had another seizure. He was in his chair, but the safety strap wasn't on. I was getting ready for my shift. And he…" Mum covered her face with trembling fingers, looking like she was about to break down. But then she lowered her hands, shook her head and took a breath. "During the seizure he fell. I found him on the floor when I came back in to the room. The doctors think he must have hit his head on the bench on the way down and now he's… Oh, Belle. He's in a coma."

"Mum," Belle whispered in disbelief, putting her arms around her mother as she began to shudder, her broken sobs echoing in the silent room. Belle held her tightly as her body convulsed, while Belle's heart wrenched as she absorbed the news. "It's my fault," Mum cried. "I should have been there. The safety strap should have been on. I should never have left him. What if he dies? What if I've killed him?"

"No. Mum. No. Don't say that." She kissed Mum on the forehead and squeezed her hard. "It's not your fault. You can't be there with him every second of the day, you just can't. It's not your fault. Shhh. It's okay, Mum. He's going to be okay"

"But what if he isn't?" Mum whispered, her eyes round and wet as she looked at Belle. And for a moment, Belle felt as though she was looking in to the eyes of a frightened child.

# Chapter Twenty-Three

"Come with me," he whispered, extending his hand toward her. His eyes gleamed like diamonds and his hair shone in the moonlight. With only a nod, she did as he commanded. She took his hand and stepped on to the boat.

"Come closer," he coaxed taking her hands and drawing her to him as the boat began to glide along the sleek, black water. Resting her head against his solid chest, she did as he commanded.

It was then that she noticed the strange shape of the boat: long and narrow, with two thin, wooden oars resting at its sides. It was more of a barge than a boat, like the ones used in funeral processions. Yet no one seemed to be steering it. And it was starting to move swiftly, as though something underneath was propelling it forward. Something didn't feel right.

"Don't panic," he said softly against her ear, sensing her alarm. He pulled the hair away from the nape of her neck and pressed a kiss against her skin, making her tremble. "We're going on a little ride."

She looked over her shoulder to see her mother by the side of the river, holding something white in her hands that reflected the light of the moon. Her eyes were sad and sunken as she held up the object for Belle to see. It was her sketchbook. She had nearly forgotten it, had nearly left it behind.

Mum opened the book and inside it, on the first page, was a mirror. Only the person she saw reflected on its surface wasn't her. It wasn't Belle. But how could that be?

Then a piece of paper slid from between the pages and floated to the ground. When it landed, Belle could see that it was a drawing she had done of Sidney, beautiful little Sidney, with his bright smile and wise eyes shining out at her from the page. Her heart wrenched at the thought that she might never see that smile again.

The boat was pulling her further and further away and she could no longer see her mother or the mirror she held. Belle scrambled to her hands and knees and looked over the edge of the boat, down at the black water. Her reflection stared back at her, a stranger with bright hazel eyes and long, strawberry-blonde hair and Belle gasped in shock. Her hands began to shake as she reared back from the stranger's image. She got to her feet and suddenly he was holding her by the shoulders, guiding her slowly until she was facing the front of the boat. They were hovering on the edge of a waterfall, going neither forward nor back, as though suspended in time. She had only to step off the end of the boat and she would plummet to her death.

"Jump," he whispered seductively, his breath warm against her ear. And then he pulled away, leaving her cold. The night wind swept along her neck, tousling her hair, and she shivered.

And without hesitating, she did as he commanded.

\*\*\*

The breeze from the window woke her. Her eyes opened and the first thing she saw was the blood red leaves of the maple tree, spiraling to the ground through the crisp, autumn air. Belle shivered, her room had become cold during the night. Her first thought was not of her brother, alone in his friendless hospital room, but of Noah, the leaves reminding her of what was to come, of what could not be changed.

Belle sighed and stretched her arms over her head. She felt stiff from huddling up during the night and unsettled from the strange dream that she couldn't quite remember. Though she didn't usually drink it, she found herself craving a nice, hot cup of coffee.

She had taken the day off school to visit Sidney. She made herself a light breakfast and was about to phone her mother to see when she should expect to be taken to the hospital when there was a knock at the door. Belle frowned, wondering who could be visiting at such an early hour on a weekday morning.

She opened the door and took a startled step back. Noah was standing on the front porch with his hands behind his back and a strange look on his face.

"Belle. Are you all right?"

She couldn't answer as her breath had caught in her throat.

"Of course you're not," Noah muttered, stepping forward to embrace her. "Mrs. Bowser told us what happened in class this morning. I'm so sorry. How is he? How are you?"

Belle closed her eyes, overwhelmed by his presence, by his words. "I'm okay," she whispered, the smell of his skin reminding her of the night they had shared. She exhaled harshly and stepped away.

"How did this happen? Is he going to be all right? God, I had no idea. So that's why you run off every afternoon. Why didn't you tell me about your brother?"

"Would you have cared?" Belle murmured, hanging her head. The secret she had tried to keep was now out in the open. She had no idea how to feel or what to think.

Noah said nothing. He raked a hand through his hair and released a slow breath. "What can I do? Is there somewhere I can take you?"

"No. Mum said she'd be back this morning. I came home to pack some of Sid's things. She should be here in an hour or so. You don't need to be here. You should be at school."

Noah looked at her as though she were mentally unsound. "School? I don't give a damn about that."

Belle found herself staring at him in amazement.

"Don't look at me that way. I'm not made of stone. You of all people..." he trailed off, dropping his eyes to the floor. "Anyway. I'm here now. I'll go when your mum gets here if you like. But we can, I don't know. Do you want to talk or something?"

The sight of Noah standing there, looking so uncertain and awkward, offering to talk, was so out of the ordinary that Belle nearly giggled.

"I saw that," Noah snapped, shoving his hands in his pockets. He made an exasperated sound. "I'm trying to help. Is that so hard to believe? But if it's all the same to you, I'll go."

"No." Belle grasped his wrist as he moved to leave. "I'm sorry. Thank you. Really."

Noah's expression softened. He stepped aside and pulled up a chair at the table, slinging one arm over the back of it as he looked around the kitchen. "So this is the Quinn residence. Cinderella's homestead. It's..." he trailed off as Belle slanted him a warning look, "...cozy." He finished with an impish grin. "Yes. Cozy. So where are the other rooms, if there are any. Where's your room?"

Belle hesitated. But Noah was looking at her expectantly so she sighed, inclining her head to the hallway to her right. "Down there."

"Well?" Noah grinned." Lead the way."

***

It felt awkward having Noah in her room. He seemed too large for it, like a giant sitting on her narrow, single bed. To his credit, he didn't comment on the state of disarray, the mismatched furniture or the shelf of stuffed animals she'd kept since childhood.

"So..." Noah began and Belle wondered if he was feeling uncomfortable as well. "Your brother. He has cerebral palsy, right? Has he always had it?"

Belle nodded. "Yeah. He was born with it. But it's only been lately that he started having seizures. I mean, he had one or two before. But years ago."

"Uh-huh. So that's a part of the disease, then?"

"In some types of CP, yeah."

"So it's another seizure. That means he'll be all right?"

Belle lowered her head, feeling the weight of the uncertainty pressing down on her chest. She couldn't bring herself to say that Sidney might never wake up. That she might never see her brother's smile again.

"Oh," Noah murmured. "I didn't know. I'm sorry."

"No, no," Belle blinked back the tears, determined to stay positive. "No, he'll be fine. He has to be. He's in a coma. I mean... that sounds bad but he could come out of it. He could..."

Noah placed a hand on her knee. "Of course he could. It happens every day. I'm guessing you're close to him?"

Belle squeezed her eyes shut and took a deep breath, nodding. Maybe talking about it wasn't a good idea. It didn't seem to be making her feel any better at all. When spoken out loud, the words sounded so harsh and made the situation seem more real.

"And that's why every afternoon... you come here, don't you? You look after him."

Belle nodded again, keeping her head down, wishing Noah would stop. She didn't want to think about what she would miss if anything happened to her brother. She couldn't bear the possibility.

"You are such a good person," Noah whispered, reaching out to tuck a tendril of hair behind Belle's ear. Tears filled her eyes. Belle wasn't used to receiving compliments. And this one had come from Noah, of all people. "I don't know how you've done it. But I'm in serious danger of falling for you." He traced a thumb along her cheek and leaned toward her, his breath warm against her face. Belle went perfectly still, unable to believe what she had heard. And then she trembled as his lips brushed hers.

I've been here before, she thought dimly through the roaring in her ears. Either this is a trick or he doesn't realize what he's doing. If I give in, I will only be hurt. Fighting the instinct to respond, she pressed her hands against Noah's chest and pushed. "Noah. I don't think…"

Noah's lips paused against hers. "Maybe you shouldn't think."

"I have to," Belle whispered hoarsely. "You don't understand. I can't."

Noah pulled back and looked at her, a flash of hurt clouding his features. But before she could blink, he had composed himself. "You're right. I'm sorry," he said, his voice devoid of emotion. And as he spoke, Belle felt something wrench inside her, something that made her want to scream "I take it back." She had never wanted anything more in her life than she wanted to kiss Noah at that moment. Before she could stop herself, she was reaching for him, her hand grasping the material of his shirt.

"Noah."

He turned to her and seeing his expression made her catch her breath. Written on his face was a mixture of pain, fear and the most startling of all, desire. He must have read something similar in her face because, in one swift movement, he cradled her face in his hands and then his mouth was on hers.

Belle felt her heart stop. Heat filled her and spread. Then she wound her fingers in Noah's hair and returned the kiss as though her life depended on it. It felt different this time, electric and desperate. They kissed feverishly at first, then slowly, deeply. Noah moaned and the sound thrilled her, and made her ache in a fierce, strange way.

He lowered her on to the bed, his hands running down her body. Belle clung to him, pressing herself against him, kissing his neck, his shoulder, feeling control slipping away. The only thing that mattered was feeling this way. She whimpered as his mouth whispered across her collarbone, down the neckline of her dress. His hand was at the hem of her skirt, creeping up. Her own hands went to the collar of his shirt and she began to pull at it, her fingers trembling as she fumbled with the buttons. Her only thought was to get as close to him as possible. She wanted to touch his skin, to feel it against her, to feel his heart beating with life.

Their mouths fused once more, charged with desperation, then all of a sudden they parted and Belle gasped, stunned by what she was feeling. They stared at each other, both wide eyed and panting, and as she read the shock on Noah's face, Belle was terrified that he would stop, that he would realize what he was kissing *Arabella Quinn* and would run screaming from the room.

But he smiled, looking extremely pleased and he leaned in to whisper in her ear. "I didn't know you had it in you," he teased and Belle sighed with relief, feeling warm and giddy and proud that she had pleased him. Noah tilted her chin up with his finger and was bending to kiss her again when they heard the doorknob turn and the sound of the hinge creaking. Noah leaped back with lightning speed and Belle sat up as her mum entered the room.

"Oh." Mum started when she saw Noah sitting on the bed. Her shrewd gaze ran from Noah's half un-buttoned shirt to her daughter's bright eyes and swollen lips. "Well," she breathed. "I was going to give you an update on your brother's condition, but if you're busy..."

"No, Mum," Belle scrambled to her feet and ran a hand through her tangled hair. "We're not. Tell me, please. We were just..."

"Yes, I can see what you were just," Mum said dryly with a stern glance at Noah. He had the grace to look sheepish as he stood quickly and straightened his shirt.

"Uh." Belle gestured awkwardly. "This is Noah."

"I gathered that," Mum responded. "Nice to finally meet you, Noah."

"Likewise," he said, stepping forward to extend his hand. "How is your son? I was sorry to hear about what happened."

Mum nodded and gave his hand a brief shake. "Well, it's not good news or bad news, love. He's stable. There's a possibility he'll come out of the coma. But there's also a possibility that he won't. So we'll have to wait and see."

"Mum. He's going to be okay. I know it. He's strong, he's going to beat this." Tears stung Belle's eyes as she put her arms around her mother and gave her a squeeze, not knowing if she believed her own words.

"Of course he will, baby Belle," Mum said. "He has to."

# Chapter Twenty-Four

"Is this a joke? Or am I going to wake up any minute and find that I've dreamed all this and you've left something vile on my pillow or something?"

Noah threw back his head and laughed. The unexpected sound was startling. "Of course not. Well, I hadn't thought of that, actually, but no. No joke. Nothing vile. We can give it a try, Belle," he said persuasively, leaning over her as she stood against the library wall. He smiled as he coiled a strand of her hair around his finger. "I know I've been... well." He sighed, looking down at his shoes. "I'm ashamed to think of it now. I don't deserve your trust. But yesterday..." he let out a low whistle, making Belle blush. "Don't you think we might have a shot at something here? We could at least give it a try. Tell me we can."

Belle shook her head in amazement, still grappling with the concept of Noah Cole asking her to "give it a try" with him. She didn't dare look in to his eyes, knowing that she could refuse him nothing if she did. Even if it meant signing the consent to her own demise. "I don't know, Noah. I mean, what's the catch? Seriously. And what about your mother? What she wanted for you? And when June comes, you'll be leaving. This can never work out. I mean, there's no real future for us."

Noah leaned in and pressed a kiss to her earlobe, causing her to jump. "Perhaps not. But I know how I feel right here, right now. And it'll be awfully fun while it lasts."

Belle shivered as his breath warmed her skin. "Noah," she replied breathlessly. "Fine. I'll think about it. But stop now so I can get to class."

"In a minute," he whispered, kissing her neck, his hands sliding down her back. He removed his lips from her throat and kissed her mouth and she felt hot and dizzy as though all the blood had rushed to her head.

"Noah." She tried to pull away, glancing over his shoulder as a group of students walked by. "Stop. Someone will see us."

"Let them look," he said, tracing her cheek with his thumb. He kissed her again and this time she gave in, sliding her hands in to his thick hair and opening her mouth to his. They kissed until her heart was thudding wildly, until her cheeks were flushed and she felt drugged with pleasure. When Noah pulled back she was out of breath and felt the insane urge to blurt out that she loved him.

"There might be a future," Noah panted, his eyes heavy-lidded as he smirked at her. "On one condition."

Belle groaned. An ulterior motive as usual, she thought, breathing deeply to try to slow her racing pulse. It was going to take some time getting used to kissing Noah. "I knew there'd be a catch. Whatever it is, I'm sure it's a bad idea."

"Don't you want to hear what it is? Surely you're curious?"

Belle was about to protest, but then she stopped and bit her lip. She was curious. What condition could possibly change whether or not they had a future together?

"Go on then. What is it?"

Noah drummed his fingers against his chin as he looked at Belle and, she imagined, her current stare of disarray.

"Maybe we can make something of you, Arabella Quinn."

# Chapter Twenty-Five

Belle was beginning to feel like Eliza Doolittle. The makeover and new clothes were one thing, but having her hair cut was quite another. The haircut been agreed upon after much discussion, and protests, but Belle still wasn't sure she was comfortable with the whole idea.

"Haven't I been right so far?" Noah raised an eyebrow as Belle reluctantly sat down in the swivel chair. "You like all your new clothes, don't you?"

Belle sighed and nodded, looking down at her flowing, off-the-shoulder olive green dress. The strappy suede shoes were uncomfortable and the off-the-shoulder sleeves were annoying, but she did look good, at least. It was all happening too fast though.

Noah grasped the arms of the chair and whirled her around to face herself in the mirror. "Now imagine what that pretty little face will look like when you can actually see it." He lifted the hair back from her face and raked it in to a makeshift ponytail. Belle gave a shy smile as he kissed her cheek.

She couldn't help but compare them as she looked at their reflections. His tanned skin against her paleness, his golden hair against the vibrant red of hers. She looked so peculiar beside him and she couldn't deny that a part of her ached to look like she belonged with him. Maybe he was right. Maybe it was finally time to let go of her veil and step out in to the light.

She took a deep breath and met Noah's eyes in the mirror. "Okay. Let's do it."

***

"Oh my God." Mum exclaimed, clutching a hand to her chest as though she were having a heart attack. "Belle? For a second I didn't know it was you."

Belle dropped her head . "It's me, Mum."

"Oh my," Mum breathed, her eyes round with wonder as she stepped forward and picked up a strand of Belle's sleek, straight, shoulder-length hair. She stared at the strand for a few seconds then stepped back and ran her eyes over her daughter from head to toe. "Why? I mean, how?"

I thought it was time for a change," Belle said with a shrug, scrutinizing her mother's expression. "Do you like it?"

Mum didn't say anything for a moment and Belle felt a stab of panic. But then Mum's eyes moistened and she shook her head, blinking rapidly. "I can't believe it. You look so different. You're beautiful, darling."

Belle released the breath she'd been holding and sighed with relief. "Really? Do you think so?"

Mum dabbed at her eyes with a hanky. "Would I say so if I didn't? I mean, you always were beautiful, of course. But you look like you stepped out of a magazine or something. How did you afford all of this?"

Belle bit her lip. She'd been dreading that question. "Um…you're not going to like it, Mum. But it was all Noah."

Mum's head shot up. "Belle. Don't tell me he paid for all of this? You know how I feel about accepting charity."

"I know Mum, I know. And I didn't want to accept it, believe me. It wasn't charity, exactly. This was all his idea. And I'm paying him back, I swear. A small amount every month. I told him I would, and I'll find a way."

The crease in Mum's forehead softened. "I suppose that's not so bad as long as you pay him back."

"I will." Belle vowed. "Of course I will."

Mum planted her hands on her hips. "You'd better," she said firmly. But within seconds the stern look dissolved in to a watery smile.

"What?" Belle asked warily, unaccustomed to seeing such an expression on her mother's face.

"Oh, baby Belle. You look like a real, live princess."

# Chapter Twenty-Six

Sidney's cheek felt cool when Belle kissed it. It surprised her, and she lifted a hand to touch his brow. Then she pulled the covers up a little higher and sat on the edge of the bed, taking his hand in hers.

"I have so much to tell you," she whispered, stroking his hand gently. Tears welled in her eyes and she blinked them back, appalled by her weakness. If there were any possibility that Sidney could hear her, he wouldn't want her to start blubbering. She swallowed firmly.

"Do you like my new hair? It was a shock at first. But I think I'm used to it now. It's much easier to manage. And it's thinner, so I don't get so hot..." she trailed off, wondering if it was a sane thing to do, talking to someone who probably couldn't hear her. But then she looked at her brother's smooth, pale face and decided that she didn't care.

"Noah and I are seeing each other," Belle smiled a little as she told Sidney. "I think we are, anyway. It's strange, Sid. I wish I could explain it, but I can't. It just happened. I'm not sure why, or even how, really. I guess he likes me. Or he wouldn't have..." Again, Belle paused, realizing something as she spoke aloud. She wanted to believe that Noah liked her, that he had her best intentions at heart. But she couldn't be sure. He had hurt her more than once and now he was treating her so differently.

Before, she had been safe. She could keep her distance. But now, things were changing so quickly, and so was she. By becoming involved with Noah, was she risking more of herself than she should?

Belle sighed, lifting Sid's hand to her lips and kissing it. "You'd know what to do, wouldn't you?" she whispered. "You always know what to do." She looked down and pulled on the golden chain and withdrew the ring from the neck of her dress. "He asked me to keep this," she said softly, holding the gleaming ring near to Sidney's face. "It was his father's and he asked me to keep is safe for him. It's more precious than you could ever imagine, Sid. And it's a secret. Only he and I know. And now, so do you." Belle smiled softly, reaching out to stroke a finger across her brother's cheek. She swallowed the lump in her throat as she looked at his unresponsive face. He was so pale and thin that he looked more of a child than he had in years.

"Sid," Belle whispered, feeling an ache so deep and so hollow in her chest that she thought it would swallow her up. She lowered her cheek against his chest, listening to his steady heartbeat, and began to weep silently. "Please wake up. If you can hear me, please, *please* wake up. We need you here. *I* need you. Please don't leave me."

# Chapter Twenty-Seven

The world was a different place on the arm of Noah Cole. People were polite, generous and went out of their way to be nice to them. At restaurants, they were seated wherever Noah requested. And wherever they went, they were looked at, attended to and treated with kindness and respect.

Belle was beginning to suspect that maybe her new hair and clothes had something to do with the change as well. It was a strange feeling to accept that people weren't staring because of her ridiculous hair, mismatched clothing or freakish height. They were staring because she looked good. When the fact dawned on her, Belle had to pause to recover her senses.

The reception she got at school had been by far the strangest. People hadn't recognized her at first. And when they did they stared. A lot. They whispered and made approving sounds. Anastasia had scowled, first at Belle and then at Noah, and pointedly turned her attention elsewhere. But no one laughed, as she had feared. In fact, nobody said anything. Even Susie.

When they locked eyes in the playground one morning, Susie's eyes bulged and she nearly choked on a mouthful of water. Belle smiled and was about to greet her when Susie's eyes hardened and she turned away. Hurt, Belle hovered for a moment, wondering whether to go and speak to her friend, to explain everything so that she would understand. But then Susie shook her head and walked away.

The hardest part of being at school was keeping her hands off Noah. Or, more accurately, keeping Noah's hands off her. When she least expected it, he would sneak up behind her, slide his arms around her waist and kiss the back of her neck. She would be working on something in art and he would waggle his brows and make eyes at her from across the room. They would be in assembly and he would lean over and whisper suggestive things in her ear, making her blush. He was driving her crazy and yet she couldn't seem to get enough.

"You know, Cinderella," Noah said conversationally, toying with a strand of Belle's glossy hair as they lay on the grass near the tennis courts. "This whole makeover thing has worked out so well, I'm thinking you might be ready for the next step."

"Next step?" Belle propped herself up on her elbow. She narrowed her eyes. "I don't like the sound of that."

"Hear me out," Noah chuckled, drawing her against him and pressing his lips to hers. After permitting this for a moment, Belle pulled away and caught her breath.

"What step?"

"Oh, I don't know." Noah smiled lazily. "In terms of planning for the future. We're almost half way through the year already. Have you thought about university applications?"

Belle pursed her lips, staring at a thatch of crabgrass that was growing through the freshly mown lawn. "I hadn't planned to go to uni," she admitted. "You know we can't... I mean, my family can't afford it."

"It wouldn't be a problem," Noah said curtly and Belle understood his meaning at once.

"Absolutely not," she insisted, sitting up and brushing the grass from her clothes. "That's the most ridiculous thing I ever heard. You can't. You know I could never let you do that."

Noah lifted his hands in defense. "Did I say a word?"

"I know what you were going to say."

"All right." Noah laughed, tugging her hand until she relented and lay back down beside him. "You got me. I'm *suggesting* you may want to let me support you through uni. If you're serious about a future together, I think you should consider it. It could mean you'll get a great job, and have a bright future. You could become the kind of woman... Well, let's say you could break the cycle. For you, and your family. Would that be so bad?"

Belle lowered her eyes, wishing desperately that Noah Cole wasn't so skillfully persuasive. He was offering her the world and making it sound like it was nothing more than a small favor. And he was using what he knew would get to her, the prospect of helping her family, and of losing him if she did not consent to his terms. Once more, she wondered what was at stake.

"I have thought of that," she confessed. "Many times. Going to uni, making something of myself in order to help my family."

"Then why don't you?"

Belle sighed. "It's not as simple as that. I had a plan, years ago. I planned to study medicine, like Susie. I thought that if I could become a doctor, all our problems would be solved. I could use my knowledge and skills to help Sidney while making enough money to support all of us. Believe me, I've thought about the possibilities over the years to the point of obsession."

"So what's stopping you?"

Belle laughed. "Are you kidding? Do you know how long it takes to become a doctor? How many hours of study and years of internship? I'd never have time for Sidney. Or work. And what if I failed? I'm not cut out for that kind of life. And then all the other options that would qualify me for high-paying jobs... I'm not competitive enough. I'd be better off working at the pharmacy, helping to support Mum and Sid. That's what Mum wants me to do, anyway."

"You don't have much confidence in yourself, do you?" Noah pinned Belle with his iridescent gaze and she felt as though he was seeing straight through her. "Have you always done what everyone else tells you to do?"

Belle looked down. "It's not like that. Uni is so expensive these days. We could barely afford textbooks, let alone all the fees, and that's with assistance. Plus. Mum needs my help. It makes more sense for me to work."

"Well if you don't mind my saying so, that's rather short sighted. You'd have to make some sacrifices, certainly, but you'd be securing yourself a future. I think you should consider my offer."

Belle took a deep breath. "I'm not about to accept charity from you, Noah. Besides, it's not like I don't have a plan B. If I make it in to the exhibition with my art this year, I can give half the prize money to Mum and the rest I can put towards studying fine arts. Yes, I know, I know. The chances are slim. It's unlikely it will get me anywhere in the long run. But all it takes, is getting noticed by one person. One contact. If the curator of an Art Gallery likes my work, who knows what could happen? And this is one thing I know I can do. It's the only thing I've ever been able to do right."

Noah didn't say anything. He ran his eyes over Belle's earnest face and for a moment he softened. "Sweet Belle. It's a lovely thought. Really. But you're fooling yourself if you think it wise to put all your faith in a dream. You certainly have talent, but so do many out-of-work artists. And there's so much more at stake here, specifically, your family's livelihood. Not to mention us. Tell me you'll think about studying something a little less risky."

"It's not off the cards, I guess," Belle said carefully, sighing. She tried to ignore the thrill that had gone through her when he had said "us," and the nagging suspicion that there was more to Noah's plans than he was sharing with her. "But there's no way I'd ever let you pay my way through uni. Not in a million years. I already owe you so much for everything you've given me. I won't accept it, Noah. If I am to go to uni, I'll get a job working more than only Sundays. And I'll rack up a massive debt."

Noah began to protest but Belle, panicking at the prospect of hearing one more persuasive word, clapped a hand over his mouth. "No. This is one thing that I'm putting my foot down, Noah." She removed her hand in time to see him grin widely.

"Oooh, putting your foot down, are you? This is a side of Ms. Quinn I've never seen. I like it."

Belle rolled her eyes and slapped at his hand as he reached for her. "Do we have a deal, or not?"

"Hmmm. You drive a hard bargain. A law degree would be right up your alley. And I suppose, if it means I get to keep you..." he smile, his eyes softening. "Perhaps we could work something out."

"Law?" Belle exclaimed. "You never mentioned anything about doing law. I don't think..."

"Hush," Noah drew her close and covered her lips with his. "You think too much. We'll work that out later." And Belle forgot what she was going to say as she gave herself over to sensation.

"Get a room," Ben jeered as he, Daniel and Brianna approached them. Belle pulled free of Noah's embrace, but Noah seemed unmoved by the interruption.

"We would, but the study room was occupied by Daniel and your mother," he returned smoothly.

It was a moment before Ben understood his meaning and then his face began to turn red. He glanced at Daniel and then back at Noah. "Hey. What'd you say about my mum?"

Noah held up his hands and laughed softly. "I'm kidding, Carter. So, we still on for tonight?"

Ben furrowed his brow, clearly struggling to figure out what had had happened. He cleared his throat. "Uh, yeah. Yeah. That's what we came to ask you. You guys in?"

Noah inclined his head towards Belle. "Do you want to come for a ride?"

"A ride? In your car? I don't know."

Noah grinned and turned back to Ben. "Yeah, we're in."

"We still get to take it for a spin?"

"If you're lucky." Noah smirked. "We'll see how well you travel as a passenger first. You might want to bring a change of underwear."

"What?" Ben knitted his eyebrows together. "Why?"

"When it happens, you'll know."

# Chapter Twenty-Eight

Belle felt as though she were in a movie. With the music blaring from the stereo, the crisp autumn air blasting against her face and a carload of friends laughing and singing and making a racket, she felt a sense of freedom that she had never known before. In pride of place in the front seat next to Noah, it felt as though she had finally found somewhere to belong.

Belle clung to the edge of her seat, her heart thundering as they flew around street corners and screeched down the long, winding country road that led to the coast. As Noah glanced over at her and smiled she felt something warm and tingly spread through her body like a drug. And when he let go of the gear stick to give her knee a quick squeeze she thought she would die of happiness.

They left the car in Noah's driveway and headed down to the water with a cooler full of beer and a couple of bottles from the beach house cellar. Brianna giggled, confessing that the champagne had gone straight to her head and even Anastasia seemed friendlier after several guzzles. The six of them set up their makeshift picnic and an iPhone with mini speakers under the pier, creating a relaxed, summery sort of atmosphere in the middle of autumn.

"That's a weapon of a car, Cole," Daniel said admiringly, throwing back the dregs of another beer. "What sort of engine has it got in it?"

"I'll show you if you like," Noah offered and Daniel jumped at the chance. "You guys want to see it?"

"I do." Anastasia squealed, scrambling to her feet. She grabbed Brianna's hand and pulled her along with her. "You coming, Carter?"

Ben cast a lazy eye over Anastasia's sleek, model-like figure. "Nah. I'm pretty cozy right here." He grinned at Belle and held up his beer in salute. "You gonna keep me company, Quinn?"

Belle hesitated. She couldn't help but feel pleased that she had been bestowed a nickname like the others, and one that wasn't derogatory. But she was still wary of Ben after years of being bullied. She looked to Noah but he was already heading up the sandy slope with the others in tow. "Sure," she said with a tentative smile. "Why not?"

Ben sighed contentedly as he popped the lid off his fourth beer. "I reckon I misjudged you, Quinn," he slurred as he stretched out beside her on the sand. The breeze from the water was cold and without the aid of alcohol to warm her, Belle sat up and hugged her knees to her chest. "You're a good sort. A good girl."

Belle ducked her head, thinking that people behaved quite strangely when they had been drinking. Did he really mean what he said or was it the alcohol talking?

"I mean, I know I used to give you crap. I feel bad about that, y'know? But it was all in good fun. And you were different then."

Belle bit her lip. Had she really been so different? Underneath she felt the same as she ever had. What had really changed aside from her clothes and her hair? And the fact that she was attached to a certain someone.

"You could give princess Anastasia a run for her money now, I reckon." He chuckled, leaning over on one elbow so that he was facing her. "She's been a pill since Cole gave her the flick. And Brianna's gone all cold on me, y'know? She used to be fun. But now..." he looked over Belle's shoulder and she followed his gaze to see Brianna and Daniel walking back hand in hand. "Well, you get the picture."

Belle looked back in time to see a scowl slide over Ben's lips and she understood immediately. It occurred to her how complicated their lives were, more than she had imagined. It wasn't all fun and games for the beautiful people. It was a strange, layered world rife with jealousy and competition. And it seemed that Ben no longer wielded most of the power.

Something about this caused Belle to panic. Noah had been gone a while and only Brianna and Daniel had returned. And that meant that Noah was with Anastasia.

"Wanna glass of bubbly?" Ben asked, pulling a half empty bottle from the cooler. He rifled around, looking for a plastic wineglass.

"No thanks," Belle said quickly. "I'm not eighteen yet."

"Aw, c'mon," Ben laughed, finding a glass and holding it out to her. "Neither is Brianna. It's no big deal. Maybe the old you didn't drink, but the new one might."

But Belle was too distracted to worry about having her first glass of champagne. She couldn't stop imagining what Noah might be doing with Anastasia. Daniel and Brianna had disappeared and Noah had left her to fend for herself. Again.

He never promised her anything, she reminded herself sternly. He hasn't told you he loves you. All he said was, "It'll be fun while it lasts." What if the fun is already over?

"Yoo hoo, earth to Belle." Ben was calling in a singsong voice. "Aw, you look all worried. Come on, have some champers, it'll loosen you up."

Belle eyed the glass, considering it for a moment. Alcohol did seem to make people looser.

"Come on," he coaxed, reaching over to put his hand on her knee. "You'll feel good. I promise." Belle stared at the hand on her knee as it began to slide slowly up. "Don't you want to feel good, Belle?"

Belle's mouth opened but no sound came out. She felt paralyzed with surprise and sudden trepidation.

"Come on, babe," he leaned in and she could smell the sour twang of alcohol in the air between them. "Just a little sip?"

"She said no, Carter," a voice said from nearby and both Belle and Ben jumped. Ben withdrew his hand and scrambled to his feet.

"Hey," Belle breathed with relief, standing up as Noah stepped out from the shadows. "You're back."

"And none too soon, I gather," he replied dryly, casting an eye over Ben's retreating form. "I can't leave you alone for a minute, can I Belle?"

Belle's eyes widened. "Excuse me? I wasn't…"

"That's not what I meant." Noah looked at Belle's stricken face and his expression softened. "Maybe it will take a while for you to get used to this new life." He stepped closer and drew her in to his arms. "I keep forgetting. Maybe I need to be more careful. Perhaps I'm corrupting you." He chuckled but the sound held no humor.

Belle sighed against his chest as she admitted he might be right. But what if she didn't want to get used to this world? What if things had been easier the way they were?

Noah was silent on the way to Belle's place after they had dropped the others home. When they pulled up outside her house he turned to her and kissed her gently. Then he held her face and whispered in her ear. "You're mine," he said, the strength in his voice causing her to start.

"Am I?" she breathed, thinking of Anastasia, of Noah's prolonged absence and the promises he hadn't made.

"Yes," he murmured, raining kisses on her face. "Mine. My Arabella." And he kissed her soundly until she couldn't think, until her heart raced and her face grew hot and everything began to tingle.

*So I am his. But is he mine?*

# Chapter Twenty-Nine

"Come closer," he whispered and she looked down to see that the black water was drifting past once more, lapping gently at the sides of the boat. Her feet were bare and they felt cold against the smooth, dark wood.

"Do you trust me?" he asked, holding out his hand and showing his perfect teeth in a smile. She felt dazzled and heartsick at his beauty, but something clawed at her stomach and tingled down her spine, something that told her to look behind her.

Ignoring his outstretched hand, she turned to see a tiny figure jumping up and down on the banks of the river. As she peered at it, the figure seemed to come closer and all at once she saw that it was Sidney. He was waving frantically and smiling, his beautiful, happy little smile, and Belle's heart leapt. He was awake. He was awake and he was okay. She knew at once that she had to go to him.

"Belle," a deep voice warned from behind her but she was already stepping off the edge of the boat and in to the river. She found that it was shallow and she began to run through the sleek, black ripples, toward the flailing arms of her brother.

"Sidney." she called delightedly. "Sidney, I'm coming." But even as she ran, he seemed to be getting farther away. She pumped her legs faster but, to her frustration, the same thing happened. And then a figure appeared beside her brother, a little girl of about seven or eight, with wild strawberry colored hair and ice blue eyes. She looked at Belle with a sad, sunken expression and reached out to take Sidney's hand. Sidney stopped and turned to the girl. And then, with a glance over his shoulder at Belle, he turned and they began to walk away.

"Wait," Belle screamed, struggling desperately to move forward though she never seemed to get any closer. "Sidney. Please, wait."

Sidney looked at the girl and she nodded. They both smiled and turned slowly to face her. "You can still help us," the girl said, her words as clear as if they had been spoken in her ear. "You can still help us."

***

It had been nearly a month since Sidney had gone in to hospital and there were six weeks remaining until Noah's eighteenth birthday. Those were the two most prominent thoughts in Belle's mind as she sat on her bed with her textbooks unopened in front of her, staring at the nearly bare branches of the maple tree.

It had become too cold for her to sit on her favorite branch and she had been too distracted with exams, Sidney, and Noah, to spend any time sketching, yet she felt the loss of her beloved hobby much less than she would have imagined. She supposed it was that way with everyone when they were in love, everything else seemed to pale in significance.

Every second she spent without Noah she thought of him, pined for him, dreamed of him. Belle traced the outline of the solid ring through her t-shirt, trying not to think of how much it would hurt when the dreaded day of departure finally came.

Yet something else weighed on her mind from time to time, something that had plagued her dreams more than once. Though she understood Noah's reasons for hating his father's mistress and the child she had given birth to, Belle couldn't help but wonder about them, about their impoverished lives and what might have been had Noah's mother chosen a different path and hadn't cast them out in to the cold.

Of course, Belle could understand Felicia Cole's reasons. But it seemed that because there was a child at stake, a child who, by blood, was Noah's sibling, there might be a niggling curiosity in him as to what had become of them. Surely a part of him cared. After all, the child was his half what? Belle didn't know whether Noah had a brother or a sister.

A pulse of anticipation washed over her as an idea entered her mind. She pushed her books aside and slid off the bed, padding through the hallway and in to the living room where she sat at the table and took a deep breath. She flicked the switch on the old Macintosh computer and waited while it vibrated and whirred and took its time starting up. When she had connected to the Internet and

Google finally appeared on the screen, Belle hesitated for a moment before typing in three words.

Austin Cole scandal.

After several anxious seconds, the screen filled with search results. The one at the top read: *Austin betrays Felicia with trusted family au pair* and as she scrolled down the page, all the links bore similar titles, the one at the bottom reading *Cole family tragedy – Austin Cole commits suicide after prolonged media harassment.*

There was a picture of Austin and an older version of Noah with a wide, pearly smile and eyes that leapt from the screen. But the eyes were not as icy as Noah's. They were warm and friendly looking. If Belle hadn't been told otherwise, she would have suspected that he was kind.

Belle imagined Noah's reaction when he'd first heard the terrible news. He had been eleven years old. And at such a young age, finding out that his family had been betrayed, then being hunted by the media, and receiving word of the sudden and tragic death of his father, was it any wonder Noah had ended up the way he was?

Belle shook her head, sighing sadly. As she was about to close the window, ashamed that she had pried in to Noah's private life, something caught her eye. Near the bottom of the screen a heading exclaimed *Alice Byrne speaks out for the first time about her affair with Austin Cole.* Belle felt a spark of anger. That the woman had such audacity after what the family had gone through, and all because of her. Belle clicked on the link.

After having scanned only the first few paragraphs, she learned that Alice hadn't "spoken out" as the title had advertised. The interview had been with someone who claimed to be a close friend of hers. In fact, after perusing several more articles and watching a clip of news footage, Belle discovered that Alice had refused to communicate with the media from the start, stating that she "had no intention of talking to anyone about personal matters," and that "what Austin and I shared is no one else's business."

Further reading confirmed that Austin had left nothing to his mistress, or to his daughter Lucy, and that they had both been forced in to hiding to escape the constant media scrutiny following Austin's death. They resided in Bankstown in a tiny, rundown unit and Lucy had to be home-schooled because the public system could not accommodate her. Lucy required around the clock care due to a disabling condition known as monoplegia, a rare form of cerebral palsy.

And suddenly the pity Belle had felt for the Coles was replaced by something else, something that stirred and simmered deep inside her.

Anger.

# Chapter Thirty

"Slow down." Noah laughed and caught Belle in his arms after she'd hurtled across the playground at him. But after a moment he saw she wasn't squirming with pleasure, she was trying to pry herself free.

"What's wrong?" he asked, releasing her and staring down at her flushed face.

"Sorry," Belle panted, lowering her eyes. "I was trying to find you, but I didn't see you, and I..." she trailed off, trying to reign in her emotions.

"What's happened? Is your brother okay?"

She nodded. "He's the same. It's not him. It's..." she tried to slow her breathing.

"What? What is it?"

"It's your sister."

Noah looked confused for a moment. And then his expression hardened and he drew back, folding his arms across his chest. "What do you know about my sister?"

Belle stared at her shoes. "I know that she's sick," she said softly. "I know that they can't afford to care for her or send her to school."

Noah didn't respond and Belle didn't lift her gaze to see his expression.

"You've been doing some research have you, red?" he asked curtly.

"I didn't mean to pry. I was curious."

"Curious," Noah repeated, drawing out the syllables in the word. "Well, that makes it all right then."

"After you told me what happened, I kept thinking about it. About how they were swept under the rug as though they didn't matter. I can understand why, Noah, but not when it's a child. Not when she's sick. Not when she has an incurable disease and they can't afford to send her to school. And you pretend to care about Sidney when you don't even care about your own sister."

The silence that fell between them was deafening. When Belle dared to look up she found Noah's face as hard as stone. And then she felt a surge of anger at his coldness. Didn't he care at all?

"No matter how you might have felt about Alice, surely even you can't believe that an innocent child deserves that."

She waited, but still he gave no response. What was the matter with him? And then he spoke and his soft words send a chill down Belle's spine.

"Enlighten me, Belle. To what disease are you referring? What does my sister have?"

Belle stared at him in awe. "Don't tell me you didn't know. Surely someone would have... Noah. You didn't know?"

Noah gave a brief, bitter laugh. "No. I didn't know. But thank you for breaking the news."

Belle winced as she realized what she had done. She took a step forward but Noah's arms tightened across his chest. "I'm sorry," she whispered. "I pressumed... I shouldn't have. I'm so sorry. But Noah, now that you know, doesn't it change things? Couldn't you help them? Help your sister? This could mean a new start for everyone. A second chance."

Noah unfolded his arms and placed them on his hips. He pursed his lips as he stared blankly ahead. "It does change things, Belle. It does indeed."

"Then you will help her?"

Noah turned his gaze on Belle and there was gloom in their icy depths.

"I'm sorry, but the answer is no. I can't. And I won't."

***

"Wake up," someone was whispering close to her ear. The dream in which she was floating with Sidney on a black river flickered and faded. "Belle. Wake up. Wake up."

Belle groaned and opened her eyes. "Mum?"

"I had a dream," Mum hissed, switching on the lamp on Belle's bedside table.

Belle blinked and scrunched up her face against the sudden glare. She peered at her mother in disbelief. "What? You woke me up to tell me you had a dream?"

"You know I get vibes, Belle. I've always been that way and you know I'm usually right."

Belle sighed and rubbed her eyes. "What was it about?" she asked reluctantly. Her mother did tend to have "vibes" about things, as she called them, but they were inaccurate as frequently as they weren't.

"Sidney," Mum said solemnly.

Belle lost the battle against a gigantic yawn. "Uh-huh. What happened?"

"Sidney was still asleep, years from now. And we had to decide whether or not to… you know. Keep him alive."

Belle made a sympathetic noise. "That would have been awful."

"It wasn't a walk in the park," Mum agreed wearily and Belle noticed that her mother had dark shadows under both her eyes and her skin looked sallow. Belle knew her mum hadn't had a proper night's sleep since Sidney's accident, and Belle felt a pang of guilt that she had been too preoccupied with Noah to take notice.

"Mum, I dream about him too," Belle said gently. "I think it's only natural when, well, when someone you love is unwell."

"I suppose so," Mum agreed. "But then there's you, Arabella."

Belle winced at the sound of her full name. "Me?"

"Yes. I'm not sure how else to put this, Belle, but the results of your exams… I'm a little worried."

Belle's jaw dropped. "You looked at my grades?"

Mum lowered her eyes, but then her face became stern. "I should have asked you first, I'll admit. But they were sitting there. And I was concerned. I want to make sure you're not throwing away your future over some boy."

Belle stared blankly ahead for a moment as she absorbed her mother's confession. Then she shook her head in disbelief. "They weren't that bad, Mum. They've gone down a bit, I agree, but I still passed everything."

"Listen, Bels, I don't want to blow this thing out of proportion. God knows there's enough on both our plates as it is. This is probably partly my fault. I can see now that I've been a little easier on you than I should have because I was happy to see you going out, acting like other kids your age. But I think I've let it get too far. This is your final year of school. And you've changed so much. You're spending all your time with this Noah character, who I hardly know, and I barely see you anymore. And now I find your grades are slipping. I've got enough to worry about. You know that. With Sid and work and the bills that keep coming in. Please tell me you'll buckle down and sort this out before it's too late."

Belle took a breath and fought against the urge to defend herself. She tried to be reasonable. "Mum. I don't think it's a big deal. We never planned for me to go to uni anyway, so I don't see how it matters."

"Stop." Daisy snapped, and Belle blinked in surprise. "I know that's what we said. I know I said I needed help with Sid, and that's still true. But it's too much to ask that you work, support Sid, study and pay your own way through uni. I wish I could afford to help you, Belle, I really do. I'm sorry things aren't different. But I don't want you giving up your chance of ever going to uni. And I know you want to do your art, or whatever it is you do up in that tree."

Belle looked up sharply. She hadn't thought her mother had ever noticed what she was up to and the revelation stunned her. "Mum."

"No." Mum shook her head firmly, her brown curls swishing. "I don't want you giving up your future for me or for *anyone*, you understand? If you decide you want to go, Bels, we'll find a way. We always do."

Belle stared for a moment in shock. She looked in to her mother's eyes, so wide and dark and sincere in her drawn, pale face, and the magnitude of what she was offering sank in. A lump rose in her throat. "Wow. Thank you, Mum. That really means a lot." Belle swallowed against the lump. "But if I do go, I swear I'll work too. Lots of people do it. I could work at least three or four days and still study."

Mum gave a short nod. "Well. That would be helpful, I'll admit." Her lips tweaked in the smallest of smiles. "You're a good girl, Belle. I know I've been lucky like that. But you still need to buckle down. I know an arts degree isn't rocket science, but you'll need a reasonable grade point average."

Belle nodded, smiling as she blinked back tears. "Yes, Mum."

"And then there's the other matter, of course."

"Oh?"

"You and Noah."

"Oh." Bell gulped.

"I want to make sure. You're being safe, aren't you?"

Belle furrowed her brow and Mum wrung her hands. "Don't make me explain. You know what I mean. Don't you?"

When it dawned on Belle her face flushed red. "Mum. Oh, no. No. No. No. You don't need to worry. Seriously. I promise." She felt herself burning as she stared at her hands, at the lamp, anything but her mother's face.

Mum cleared her throat. "Good. Okay. Good. I was checking. I'm your mother, you know, and I'm obliged to... well, that's settled anyway. As long as you're not... Well."

Belle felt the sudden urge to giggle but she bit down hard against it. Her mother was right to be suspicious. Though she and Noah hadn't slept together, they had come close. And it was becoming harder to delay what they both wanted. Though the knowledge that he was leaving soon made her uncertain. But, she knew that when it came down to it, she wouldn't refuse him. She wanted him and, if she was honest with herself, she always had.

Though the thought of sex with the ultra-experienced Noah Cole was thrilling and intimidating, Belle had never considered the act itself to be indecent or wrong. She wanted to express her love for him in that way, wanted to be as close to him as it was possible to be to another human being. And then the unnerving thought occurred to her that her mother might have had one of her predictive dreams about it, and the urge to laugh quickly passed.

"I can honestly tell you, Mum," Belle said firmly, but her voice faltered as Noah's beautiful, icy eyes crept into her mind. She thought of his hands on her body, his lips against her skin and she was suddenly positive that she was about to tell her mother a lie.

"You have nothing to worry about."

# Chapter Thirty-One

Sidney was showing no signs of waking up. Occasionally, his eyelids would flutter or his arm would twitch when Belle held his hand and she would nearly leap from her seat with excitement. But when she told the doctors, they explained that it was normal for coma patients to move occasionally and that it was simply the body responding to touch, movement or light. It was, however, a good sign as it meant that Sidney hadn't fallen victim to the most severe form of coma, under which the patient is completely unresponsive. Belle took some comfort in that, in some small way, Sidney was aware of her presence.

The pressures at school were starting to get to her and though Belle had passed all her exams, the strain of her personal life was taking its toll on the quality of her work. She was struggling to complete her final portrait, the urgency made stronger by her desire to secure her place in the art competition. Yet all her time was taken up by Noah or visiting the hospital, and in order to repay Noah's generosity, Belle had taken on an extra shift at the pharmacy.

What was more, Belle was growing tired of Ben Carter's company, as well as the Brianna's, Anastasia's and Daniel's. The tension with Noah remained and, despite the undeniable thrills of his attentions, Belle was finding that she was growing less and less fond of her newfound social standing.

Straightening her hair every day was a chore. Her new clothes were uncomfortable. and her fashionable, slipper-style school shoes kept sliding off at the heel. The conversation topics favored by Noah's crew were unfamiliar and not stimulating. Belle found her attention wandering more and more during their time together. And although the fine dining scene had been romantic and exciting at first, Belle couldn't help feeling that she'd prefer an intimate, leisurely meal spent at home or in a park somewhere quiet.

"Have you put any more thought in to my proposal?" Noah asked as he topped up her glass of mineral water. She knew he was referring to university applications and the pressure he'd been putting on her to do law. Though his tone was casual, Belle did not miss the expectant glint in his eye.

"Yes," Belle answered while fiddling with the hem of the linen tablecloth. She was growing uncomfortable as they kept being interrupted by overly attentive waiters and she still couldn't quite get a handle on which forks to use and when.

"And?" Noah prompted, carving a fine slice of rare steak and mopping up the remains of the red wine jus.

"And, I don't know, Noah," Belle replied, thinking of the conversation she'd had with her mother that night. "I don't know if I can."

Noah's cutlery hit the plate with a loud clink. "Of course you can. Why would you say that?"

Belle sighed, recalling why she had delayed having this conversation for so long. What was simple expectation for him was something she had agonized over, night after night, and yet could not bring herself to believe was the right path.

"There are so many reasons. First, I'd never have the time to dedicate to a law degree. It's costing a lot to keep Sidney... well, you know. I plan to work while I study. Fees and text books are ridiculously expensive."

"I understand that. But there are other options, Belle. You could get government support. Or a scholarship."

"Right," Belle scoffed. "A hundred dollars or so a fortnight? And even less if I'm working? And I'll never get a scholarship with my math grades."

Noah wiped his mouth carefully with his napkin, his eyes never leaving Belle's face. "If you're so determined to find excuses then there's always the first option. My offer."

"Oh no you don't. We've already covered that. The thing is Noah, I don't want to be a lawyer. Or a doctor, or a journalist, or anything like that."

"So you're happy wasting your time with an arts degree, knowing the chances of getting anywhere are slim to nil?"

"It's not necessarily a waste of time."

"Don't you see that you have potential to be so much more than you are?"

Belle felt as though she'd been slapped. "Then what I am isn't enough?"

"That's not what I meant."

"But that's what you said," Belle stated.

Noah sighed, and ran a hand over his face. "Belle, I'm not sure how else to say this. If you want a future together…"

"You keep saying that, Noah, but is that what you really want? You've never promised me anything."

"Well, you've never agreed to my terms."

Belle gaped at him. "Haven't I? Haven't I had all this," she gestured to the designer dress she was wearing, "done to me? Haven't I cut my hair and changed the company I keep? I don't know what more I should have to change."

Noah was silent for a moment. Then he frowned. "You know I can't consent to a future with you. Not unless you are prepared to make certain sacrifices".

Belle shook her head and sighed. "And what about your sacrifices? What are you willing to give? I asked one thing of you and you refused."

"What? What did you ask of me?"

"What? To help your sister."

Noah's frown deepened. "You know I can't do that, Belle."

"No I don't. I know you said you couldn't, but I don't know why. What could be a good enough reason to let an innocent child suffer when you have the power to do something to stop it?"

You want to know why?" Noah leaned over the table and spoke in a harsh whisper. "Because my mother asked me to make a promise, that's why. Believe me, I've thought about it over the years, wondering the same things you have. But I trusted my mother. She was all I had after I lost everything else. She knew what was best. And she would never have asked it of me unless there was a good reason. Unless there was something she knew that I didn't."

"And what could that be? " Belle asked, wondering what else his mother could have made him promise. It seemed she had asked so much of him. And he was prepared to do anything for her memory, yet so little for anyone else. "What could she know that would make what has happened to Lucy okay?"

Noah's jaw tightened. "I don't know, exactly. But it has crossed my mind that perhaps the child wasn't my father's after all. As we're all aware, Alice wasn't exactly the most moral person. Who knows whose child it could have been?"

Belle was silent as she processed his statement. "That's a possibility," she agreed. "And I understand how you feel, Noah. I do, believe me. But even if she's not your sister by blood, knowing what you know now, doesn't it mean anything to you? She's a child."

Noah's face closed up, and she could tell it was the end of the matter.

And for the first time Belle wondered whether his mother might have burdened him forever with all she had made him vow. That he's risk a lifetime of guilt should he disobey. That he might never be able to act of his own free will. If she were alive, it might be different. But it was impossible to argue with a dead woman.

Belle looked at Noah's beautiful face in the flickering candlelight, and it made him look older, more solemn, and devoid of his trademark arrogance. She stared at the sauce stain on her new silk dress and felt her breath catch as a wave of pain washed over her.

"This isn't going to work, is it?"

Noah didn't meet her gaze. If he was affected by her words, he didn't show it. He reached over and fingered the ring that rested against her chest. Then he lowered his hand to clasp her wrist, running his thumb softly over her skin. "There isn't long before I go back to Sydney. If we can't reach an agreement, do you think there might be a way to compromise? Couldn't we enjoy our time together while it lasts?"

The ache inside her grew. She knew was he was asking. It wasn't a compromise. It was an ultimatum. He wouldn't change. Things were never going to be the way she wished they could be. And he was asking her to accept it, to be with him, for today only, with no promise of tomorrow.

Slowly, Belle raised her eyes to meet his. While he was telling her what she had always known, it somehow did little to lessen the impact. And yet, strangely, nothing profound had changed. She still loved him. She still wanted him. And she found herself wondering if maybe she could be content to take what he offered.

She had never allowed herself to long for something beyond her drab little life. She'd never taken risks, or dove in to the deep end without thinking. She'd never lived only for the moment. Now was her chance.

Wasn't a brief love affair better than none at all? Or was she settling for less than she deserved?

Noah was watching her expectantly and Belle found herself smiling sadly.

"Maybe we could, Noah," she whispered bravely. She took his hand. "After all, all we have is now."

# Chapter Thirty-Two

"Beyya. Beyya." Sidney's sweet voice was calling, a plaintive plea that shivered through the darkness and into her heart.

Belle's eyes fluttered open to see Sidney thrashing violently in his hospital bed, his brow sheathed with sweat, the sheets entangled with his poor, twisted feet. She let out a moan and sprang from her chair, rushing to his side and grasping his arms with both hands.

"Sidney. Sidney? Can you hear me? You're awake, aren't you? I'm going to get the doctor. Just breathe. Just breathe." She glanced around wildly for the emergency button and when she spotted it she slammed it with her palm.

"Breathe, sweetie," she begged, staring in horror as Sidney's eyes rolled back in their sockets and he continued to convulse. She shuddered as she bit back a sob. After what felt like forever, a nurse appeared and Belle gasped with relief. "He needs help." she cried. "Please. Please help him."

But the nurse was looking at her with a strange, sympathetic smile that didn't quite reach her eyes. "I'm afraid he's gone," she said sadly, untying her hair and letting the golden locks fall about her shoulders. The nurse was Anastasia and Belle's jaw dropped in astonishment. Anastasia smiled slowly and held up her slim, elegant hand and Belle could see a diamond glinting on her left ring finger.

"What?" Belle stuttered, her eyes darting back to where Sidney lay on the bed, his little body perfectly still. "I don't understand. He was awake a minute ago." But her words were cut short as Sidney's eyes snapped open and he sat up, fixing Belle with a blank, hollow stare. Her blood ran cold. And then a hand touched her shoulder and she jumped.

"Belle," a dark voice whispered in her ear and her skin crawled with pleasure and fear. "It's time, now. It's time to let me go."

When Belle jerked awake, her chest heaving and her sheets damp with sweat, she was clutching something in her fist. And as she uncurled her fingers, she looked down at the golden ring, gleaming in the light of the moon, and her eyes spilled over with tears.

\*\*\*

The breeze whispered against Belle's neck, tousling her hair as she sat on the banks of the escarpment. Though the air was crisp, the sunset cast a warm glow over her face and she breathed deeply, gazing at the yawning expanse of purple sky.

The five of them, Belle, Noah, Ben, Daniel and Anastasia had driven to Pitts Gorge, parking the car and toting a cooler of beer, champagne and snacks down the narrow trail until they reached the lookout spot. Amid the eerie rustling of branches and the occasional magpie call, they sat and stared out to the gulf, admiring the view and chatting idly.

"So, Cole," Daniel said, taking a swig of beer. "Glad to be heading back to Sydney and out of the pits?"

Noah lifted his shoulders in a shrug. "I guess," he answered, casting a glance at Belle.

"I'd be thrilled to be getting out of this place," Brianna said wistfully, looking at Noah with envy. "Sure you don't want some company?"

"Yeah," Ben piped up. "You got a sweet pad down there, right? You could put us all up. We'd pay you rent."

Noah laughed. "Sure, Carter. You can skip exams and come work in a bar for the rest of your life."

"Hey, beats an apprenticeship any day," Ben joked, but there was a bitter edge to his tone.

"You'll stay in touch, won't you?" Anastasia asked, flashing Noah a smile. Her charm bracelet glinted in the golden light as she slid a hand through a length of blonde hair.

"Of course," Noah returned smoothly. Belle looked at him, but his eyes were cast in shadow, concealing his expression. Belle and Noah had made a pact not to contact each other, not to make their separation harder than it had to be, and she wondered if he meant what he'd said to Anastasia.

"Sucks you're gonna miss the formal," Daniel sniggered and Brianna slapped him on the arm. "Hey. I was kidding, babe, really. It's gonna be awesome."

"Yeah," Ben muttered, slanting them a sour look. "Awesome." He turned his gaze to where Belle was lying against Noah's chest with his arms wrapped around her waist. "What about you guys? Think you'll be staying in touch?"

Nobody said anything for a moment and then Noah cleared his throat. "No," he replied softly and though the words were true, Belle was hurt that he had shared that fact with the others.

"So you'll be a free woman then, will ya Quinn? Good to know." Ben sniggered and Daniel gave a token chuckle but no one else laughed. Belle felt Noah's arms tighten around her.

"And Noah will be a free man," Anastasia added sweetly. Belle looked at Anastasia's upturned face, so deceptively innocent and lovely, and wondered why she had felt the need to say what they all already knew. Did she still think she had some claim to Noah because they had once shared a kiss?

There was silence as the last dying rays of sunlight slid beneath the rocky ledge, setting the world in sudden shadow. Belle plucked up her courage and swallowed the remains of her coke. "To Noah," she said softly, clinking her glass against Noah's bottle of beer. Their eyes met and held for an infinite moment and Belle had the feeling that something she had never quite grasped was slipping from her fingers and there was nothing she could do to stop it.

Gravity would always win. And as an ache burrowed its way in to her chest she wondered, was it possible?

Could she lose something she never truly possessed?

# Chapter Thirty-Three

A single leaf clung to the top branch of the Autumn Flame as Belle walked by, shivering in the cold night air. Noah was waiting for her, leaning against his car with a rueful smile barely touching his lips as he watched her approach. Belle felt her heart squeeze a little, knowing that her own expression must reflect his. It was their last night together, the eve of Noah's eighteenth birthday.

When she reached the car, he pulled her close and kissed her until she was breathless with bittersweet longing. And when she thought it was over, he kissed her again, his hands winding possessively in her hair.

After dinner, Noah led Belle into the bedroom. The foyer seemed darker, barer, than usual and the arched doorways loomed like specters in the dim light. Her heart was heavy with the knowledge that it was the last evening she would ever spend in the Cole mansion.

As Noah took her hand and she stepped on to the staircase, she hesitated. It wasn't too late to change her mind. If she turned back, was there a chance that she could salvage her heart? And then she looked in to Noah's eyes and remembered the night he had begged her to stay. She remembered the fierce surge of love she had felt when he kissed her and held her, and she had no doubt what she wanted.

Noah flicked on the lamp by his bed and turned to Belle with a smile. "It's not too late to change your mind," he whispered, running his fingers down her arms. "I don't want you to do anything you don't want to do."

Belle lifted her chin. "I know that," she told him, nervous yet certain. "But it's what I want. I choose you, Noah."

"I'm honored," he whispered against her ear and Belle shivered. When he pulled back, the intensity in his eyes took her by surprise. "I mean it."

Belle smiled. "I want to tell you something first," she blurted before she could lose her nerve.

Noah tilted his head. "Sounds serious."

"No. Not serious, exactly. Before we... before..." she sighed, hating that she was stammering. She forced herself to look in to Noah's eyes. "You know how I feel. Don't you? You know that I...Noah, I..."

Noah pressed a quick finger to her lips. "Don't," he whispered. "Please. We agreed. Let's take this for what it is. Okay?"

Belle squeezed her eyes shut against the pain. It shouldn't have hurt. She had anticipated his response, but, still, she had wanted the chance to tell him how she felt.

"No," Noah said urgently, cupping her face. "I'm sorry. That's not what I meant. It's not because I don't... God," he pulled back, ran his hand over his face. "Why is this so hard? I'm sorry."

Belle shook her head. "It's okay, it's..."

"No, it's not. It's not okay. This is my fault. I don't know how to..." he closed his eyes as if in pain.

As she looked at Noah, it occurred to Belle that he resembled a wounded lion. His mane of hair and intense eyes spoke of danger, but also fear. To have earned his trust was one thing, but to pull out the thorn that caused him to suffer was quite another. For the first time, Belle wondered whether Noah might be more afraid of this than she was.

She took his hand. "You don't have to do anything you don't want to do," she repeated his words back to him with a smile.

Noah looked at her in surprise. Then he laughed, shaking his head. "My rare, precious Arabella," he murmured, stepping close to her. She waited, wondering if he might say something more. But then he closed the distance between them, took her hand in his and turned it slowly, bringing it to his mouth and pressing his lips to the palm.

Belle shivered and he smiled, his eyes soft. In them, she could read the words he hadn't spoken. He released her hand, and cradled her face before he pressed his lips to hers. The kiss was soft, slow. But then he made a sound deep in his throat and the kisses grew urgent.

Belle gasped as he lowered her onto the bed. He pressed his lips to her throat as he began unbuttoning her top, his hand sliding beneath the material and grazing intimately against her flesh. He murmured her name over and over, and the sound thrilled her. It felt as though he was showing her what he could not say. And so, reaching for him and sealing her lips to his, Belle vowed to do the same.

Later, Belle stirred in Noah's arms and then came awake, shocked that she had drifted off. A tingle shot through her as she felt a warm kiss on the back of her neck and then she blushed, the memory of what they had done rushing back to her in waves.

"How long was I asleep?" she whispered, noticing that the sky was well and truly black outside.

"Only ten minutes or so," Noah whispered back, his breath tickling her ear. "I was in the middle of talking and you passed out cold. I must be truly fascinating. Either that, or I really took it out of you."

Belle giggled in embarrassment. "Sorry."

"No need. I'll take it as a compliment." Noah touched his finger to her cheek and turned her gently to face him. He smiled down at her, a contented, happy smile she'd never seen before, and then he kissed her gently on the lips. Belle sighed, smiling back. "You're okay, though, aren't you?"

Belle nodded. "I'm fine. Better than fine, actually." Belle didn't know much about the subject, she could admit, but she was fairly sure that for a first time it had been pretty amazing. She blushed, remembering it all over again. They had slept together. She and Noah had made love. The fact was as bizarre as it was wonderful. Much like the act itself.

Noah smiled, seeming satisfied with her response. He stroked a strand of hair back from her forehead and sighed. "That was the perfect birthday present," he said with a grin. Then he glanced at the clock on the wall and pursed his lips. "Do you want to stay? Will your mum be okay with that?"

Some of the blissful pleasure faded. The time they had left was evaporating. She bit her lip, not wanting to choose one way or the other.

"Stay," Noah coaxed. But even as he said the words, Belle knew she couldn't. Her resolve to let him leave without a scene was crumbling fast and she knew their parting needed to be swift or she might find that it couldn't be done at all.

"I'm sorry," she whispered as a tear slid down her cheek. "I can't."

***

"Maybe there's a way," Noah said suddenly, breaking the melancholy silence as they sat in his car outside her house. The first frost was clinging to the weather-beaten fence, the icicles glistening in the moonlight like diamonds. Noah sat forward and his eyes lit up. "Come with me. Come live in Sydney. I can give you everything you ever dreamed of. An apartment in the city, fancy dinners, movie premieres, and champagne breakfasts."

Belle stared at him in disbelief. Was that what he thought she wanted? She gave a soft, bitter laugh. "Wonderful. And then what? One day you turn around and tell me you're going to marry someone else? And I just my things and come back to Pitts?"

"What do you want, Belle? A proposal?"

"No. Of course not. I'm not quite eighteen."

"Well then, what is it? What do you want?"

"I..." Belle hesitated, lowering her eyes. Then, as the truth resounded within her, she inhaled slowly and looked up. "I want to be loved for who I am, Noah. Don't you understand? I've spent weeks trying to be the girl you want me to be. And it's been wonderful, in lots of ways, it really has. But it's not me..And then you suggest that I come to Sydney to be your temporary girlfriend.

"You're asking me to give up everything. to abandon my family to be with you when you can't commit. And when there's no hope of..." Belle trailed off, sighing heavily. "I don't want to marry you right now. But one day some beautiful billionaire's daughter is going to come along and you'll... well, we both know what's going to happen, Noah."

"Belle. I never promised that this was going to last forever. No matter how I feel." His face softened as he tucked a strand of hair behind her ear. "I made a promise to my mother. You can't ask me to break it. I can't, and I won't. So unless you will consider my offer..."

Belle squeezed her eyes shut, hating the words she was compelled to speak. But it was her only chance. And she was going to say it right. "You know I would never ask you to break your promise. I know what it means to you. And I thank you for trying, in your way. But it's not enough." She exhaled as her own words rang true. "And the only other option you're giving me is to try to be something I'm not, and no matter how many changes I make, I'm never going to be the kind of girl your mother would approve of. Frankly, I'm starting to doubt anyone could live up to that kind of expectation. I might wind up a failed artist, or working at the pharmacy my entire life, but that's my choice to make. It's my life. I don't want to feel like a consolation prize. I realize now that I can't be someone else, even if who I am isn't all that special."

Something passed over Noah's face then. He lowered his eyes and was silent for a moment. When he spoke, his voice was soft. "You are special, Belle. The most special girl I've ever known. Never doubt that."

Belle's breath caught at those precious words.

"But you're right," he continued. "I shouldn't have suggested that you come with me. And I can't ask you to be someone you're not any more than you can ask me to break the vow I made. You shouldn't have to feel second best. You shouldn't have to change and nor should I. If things were different…"

Belle shuddered as the cruel reality set in. If things were different. But they weren't. And nothing they could do would ever change that.

"Then we might have lived happily ever after," she finished sadly.

"Yes," Noah sighed, drawing her to him and resting his forehead against hers. They held each other in silence for a while before he spoke again. "But I'm afraid this isn't going to have a happy ending, Cinderella."

Belle could only nod, the finality of his words clawing through her. She looked up in to the eyes of the almost-man she loved, saw them bright with hurt and regret, and felt something splinter inside her.

It was the exquisite pain of her heart breaking for the first time.

# Chapter Thirty-Four

The winter months were long and empty. It felt as though a thousand years had passed when spring returned to Pitts, though the memory of Noah's eyes burned in Belle's memory as clearly as if he had never left.

Mum had known straight away. Belle never quite understood how, but Mum knew. Belle had come home that evening, after sitting in the park for an hour and crying until she couldn't breathe, until her ribs and lungs ached. And Mum had been waiting. She switched on the porch light as soon as Belle put her foot on the front step.

"He's broken your heart, hasn't he?" she asked in a hushed voice as she saw Belle's swollen eyes and tear-stained face. Belle nodded, breaking in to violent sobs as her mother held out her arms and pulled her in to a fierce, crushing hug. "It's all right, angel," she crooned, stroking Belle's hair and rocking her gently against her chest. "Everything's going to be all right."

But Belle wasn't sure that it ever would be. In the days and weeks that followed, a deep, hollow ache took up residence within her and spread like a disease. She spent her nights crying herself to sleep and her days in a dazed, melancholy fog. The gold chain Noah had let her keep when he took back his father's ring weighed heavily on her chest as though it were made of steel, reminding her of the fateful night of his departure. It had been, the best and worst night of her life. And though part of her ached to, she would never forget it.

After a fitful sleep in late August, Belle tiptoed in to the kitchen to get a glass of water and found her mother sitting at the table in the dark with her head in her hands. Belle flicked on the light and Mu, jumped.

"Is it Sidney?" Belle asked i, her voice echoing through the silence.

Mum blinked in the fluorescent glare and Belle could see that she'd been crying.

"Mum?"

"No," Mum said, her voice sounding strange. "It's not Sidney, darl. It's you."

Belle stared at her mother, wondering if she had heard right. "Me? Why?"

"You're not all right, are you?" Daisy asked with a waver in her voice. "You haven't been all right for a long time. even before all this Noah business. I should have paid better attention. I should have noticed. I should have talked to you, spent more time with you."

"What? Mum, it's okay, seriously. Did you just get back from work? You must be really tired. Do you want a chamomile tea or something?"

"No Belle, I mean it." Mum's face crumpled as Belle watched in horror. "I failed Sidney, my baby boy, and now I've failed you. I tried. God knows I tried. But it wasn't enough. I'm sorry, Belle. I'm so sorry." Mum broke in to sobs and Belle rushed to her side and put her arms around her.

"Mum. Oh my God. No. Are you kidding? You've done so much for Sid and me. You've done more than anyone should ever have to do."

"No." Mum sniffled and wiped her face with a hanky. "I neglected you. I never meant to, but now it's so clear. After your father left the only way I could keep going was to focus on what needed to be done. Taking care of Sidney, working, making sure you were fed and did your homework. I thought I was being strong. That I was doing the right thing. But I couldn't do the hard stuff, Belle. I couldn't talk to you. I never talked to you. I left you to grow up all by yourself."

Mum drew in a shuddering breath and clung to Belle a little tighter. Patting her mother's back, Belle sat a bit shocked at what she had heard. Mum had confessed to neglect? When she had raised a daughter and a disabled child single-handed after being abandoned by her coward of a husband?

"Mum. No. You were always there for me," Belle began, but as she said the words, she had to admit, her mother was right, about one thing, at least. Mum hadn't ever talked to Belle. Not about anything profound or meaningful. And Belle had learned a lot on her own. But she had always understood that there were more important things to be done, like caring for Sidney, and working two jobs to support them.

Belle had grown to accept that she came last. That was the way of things. And as that reality seeped in to her consciousness, she felt something lift inside her, something close to pride. That she, Arabella Quinn, had not accepted second best from Noah. That a part of her had known, somehow, some way, that when it came to love she deserved to be put first.

"It'll be different from now on, baby Belle." Mum looked up at Belle with wet, brown eyes. The color Belle had always envied, and for the first time Belle saw herself in them. "Can you forgive me?"

Belle was astonished to find herself smiling. It was the first real smile that had crossed her face in nearly three months. "Mum. Of course I can. There's nothing to forgive."

# Chapter Thirty-Five

The following night, Belle remembered something. The final work for her visual arts project was due in a week's time. Naturally, Noah was no longer there to assist with the task. Not that he would care, she thought bitterly, as he was about to complete the school year a thousand miles away at snooty Sydney Grammar.

And, of course, he had finished his work despite the fact that he had never been expected to hand it in. But hers wasn't quite done yet, and if she didn't get a move on she was going to miss the cut-off date for entry in to the art competition. It was her one chance to turn her life around, to prove to herself that she could make it as an artist some day, and if she didn't take it she would never forgive herself.

She sighed, removing her last attempt from between the pages of her sketchbook and looking at the familiar lines and planes of Noah's face. The ache that dwelled within her deepened, and for a moment she was fighting tears. Then, with a twist of her lips, she snatched the paper in both hands and scrunched it in to a tight little ball.

Belle panicked and carefully un-scrunched the paper, smoothing it out against her leg. She held her breath for a moment and when she released it, her gaze fell to the bare branches of the Autumn Flame maple, rising stark and white against the stormy sky. She stared at it, thinking how lonely it looked. Was that how she looked, too? Then, with a surge of inspiration, she gathered up her sketchbook, grabbed a graphite pencil, and ran out into the cold.

It was freezing on her favorite perch, but Belle barely felt it. She closed her eyes, scarcely glancing at the page as she drew, conjuring memories in her mind. They rippled back in vivid sensation and color. The feel of Noah's lips at her throat, his hands on her skin, the smell of his breath and the taste of his mouth. She remembered the look in his eyes that night in the trophy room when he had begged her not to leave him. She remembered his soft smile after they had made love. She remembered him in his unguarded moments, when she had seen the real Noah. When she had loved him.

An hour passed and Belle's hands were turning blue from the cold. With trembling fingers, she held the paper away from her face and felt her broken heart rejoice for a moment. Noah's face was exquisite. Mournful and beautiful. He was made so not by the structure of his face but by his vulnerability. In it, she saw the real Noah. The orphaned boy who had nothing and no one, and had convinced himself that that was what he deserved.

She felt a sense of reverence as a tear slipped down her cheek. And she wondered if some day she would regret the decision they had made. If she would run to him now, after all this time, should he ask it of her.

If she could change anything, were such a thing possible, would she?

# Chapter Thirty-Six

"You came back." The words escaped her sounding rushed and desperate.

"Of course." Noah smiled. "You expected otherwise?"

Belle's heart lurched painfully as the cornflower eyes, vivid as ever, looked her over. "Yes. No," she blurted, feeling her cheeks redden. How could she explain that she had assumed she would never see him again? That she had never been convinced he felt the same as she did to begin with?

"Well, which is it?" Noah's voice was dark, a hint of a smirk quirking the corners of his lips, as he stepped toward her. He reached forward to twist a lock of her hair around his finger.

Belle's breathing quickened. She hadn't time to question where he had come from, how he had appeared in her living room, cornering her like a lion corners its prey. Her knees felt weak and suddenly she was stumbling, tripping over some invisible object and falling backward before she could grab hold of anything. She landed in an undignified heap on the couch, her legs in a gangly twist above her.

But Noah didn't laugh, as she would have expected. Before Belle could catch her breath, he was above her, his hands on either side of her face, his toned arms supporting the weight of his body as it pressed down against her. Belle gave a startled moan. Her heart was racing, she felt flushed and weak and exhilarated at once.

Noah's face was so close that his breath puffed against her mouth. His dazzling eyes, their irises almost obliterated by engorged, black pupils, were boring in to her with an intensity that sent thrills through her. Unconsciously, she lifted her chin, straining to bring her lips to his. She saw him smirk and the familiar gesture brought on a rush of love, of need, so fierce she wanted to weep.

"Noah."

"Did you miss me?"

Belle could only gasp in response as his body shifted above her, setting her nerve-endings on fire.

"Well?" he prompted gruffly.

Belle nodded, averting her eyes from his piercing gaze.

"Say it," he demanded, shifting his weight and running a hand up the length of her body to cup her face. He tilted her chin so that she was looking at him.

"I missed you." The confession brought tears to her eyes. "So much, Noah. So much."

Noah stared down at her for so long that she wondered if she'd said something wrong. But before she could question him, he grunted and lowered his mouth to hers, kissing her with bruising force.

Belle whimpered as pleasure shot through her. She clutched at his shoulders as she responded with desperate intensity. They kissed feverishly, wildly, clutching at each other until there was no space left between them. Belle lifted her legs and wound them around his waist and he groaned, breaking the kiss to trail his lips down her throat.

Belle closed her eyes, listening to her own voice as she blurted how much she had missed him, that she needed him, that she loved him, loved him so much it hurt.

"And I love you," the words she had never dreamed she'd hear rang in her ears like angels singing. "I always have. I always will."

And with a cry of joy, Belle woke up.

# Chapter Thirty-Seven

"Ms. Faye, I'd be happy to let you in if you tell me what you want with my daughter," Belle heard her mother saying through the open back door. Her ears pricked up and she tensed on her tree branch. Ms. Faye? Belle thought. Why was that name familiar? But she didn't have time to wonder before a slim, elegant figure appeared in the back doorway followed closely by Belle's flustered, pink-cheeked mother.

"Ms. Faye, I don't take kindly to being barged in on like this."

Aunt Bethany held up a finger and immediately, though she didn't quite know why, Mum was silenced.

"Miss Quinn," Aunt Bethany fixed Belle with an icy stare. "What on earth are you doing up a tree?"

Belle was so startled she nearly lost her footing. She flung down her sketchbook, scrabbled down the trunk of the tree and brushed the bark and leaves from her clothes. "Aunt Bethany. What a nice surprise."

Bethany narrowed her eyes as she took in Belle's disheveled appearance. "Indeed. I trust that you are well?"

"I am. Thank you. And yourself?"

Bethany gave a nod. "I'm fine, thank you." She seemed to hesitate for a moment and Belle wondered why she had come. Was it Noah? Had something happened? "Well, I'll make this brief. It's a matter of business only."

Belle stood, her brow furrowed, finding once more that she had to resist the urge to curtsey. "Yes?"

"Come closer, dear."

Belle hesitated before stepping forward, recalling all she had been told about Aunt Bethany. She became suddenly conscious of the golden chain she wore around her neck. It had sprung from beneath her t-shirt as she descended from the tree and was resting most obviously against her chest.

Bethany spotted the chain at once. Her hand darted out and she hooked the delicate links with her finger, squinting at it with an appraising eye. Belle held her breath.

"This doesn't belong to you," Aunt Bethany said in a low, menacing voice.

Belle started, surprised by how much the words stung. "Yes, it does. I know it was your sister's. But Noah gave it to me."

Bethany flashed her steely eyes to Belle's. "Liar."

"How dare you call my daughter a liar," Mum's stern voice came from the doorway.

Belle looked up in panic. "Mum. It's okay, I'll take care of this."

"But Belle. This woman burst in without being invited, stormed through my house and now she's accusing you."

"I will only take a minute of your daughter's time," Bethany interrupted brusquely. "I can assure you I will be gone before you know it."

Mum's expression darkened but Belle shot her a meaningful stare. "Thank you," she mouthed as her mother backed in to the house. It was only a moment before the venetian blinds at the kitchen window slid open a crack and half of Mum's head appeared.

Belle shook her head. "Sorry. You were say?"

"Tell me this once and for all, Miss Quinn. Do you have the ring or don't you?" Bethany asked, ensnaring Belle in an ice blue stare.

Belle went rigid, her senses suddenly on high alert. "No," she said stiffly. "I don't."

"I don't believe you," Bethany snapped.

Belle exhaled slowly. "You don't have to, but it's true. I don't have it."

Bethany narrowed her eyes. Then her expression changed and her lips stretched in a false smile. "You poor child," she said in a tone devoid of sympathy. "Don't be misguided by some pathetic belief that Noah is in love with you. How much can you have meant to him if he has left you here? Don't you think he'd have found himself some nice, young blonde down in Sydney by now?"

Belle kept silent as she felt a swift thrust of pain.

"Let me guess. He gave you the ring, made you promise not to tell anyone his secret, and told you he trusted you and no one else?"

Belle looked at her shoes and Bethany gave a hollow laugh. "As I thought. My devious, darling nephew. He truly does take after his father. Tell me, Arabella. Do you think it's fair that the ring should stay in the Cole family after everything Austin did to dear Felicia? Do you think my sister would have wanted to see Noah make the same mistakes as his father?"

"He was her son," Belle said softly. "She would have wanted him to have it."

"Don't be so naïve," Bethany snapped. "You know nothing of what went on in that family. Felicia wanted me to have the ring. She confided in me before she died that it would be a mistake to give Noah the kind of power his father had. That it would go to his head and ultimately destroy him the way it destroyed Austin.

"But she died before she could change the will. I tried to reason with the solicitors but they don't care what's fair or true, only what is there, written out in black and white. Does that mean that dear Felicia shouldn't get what she wanted most? Ask yourself that, Miss Quinn. And if there's an ounce of sense in that lovesick little head of yours you'll do what's best for Noah and grant his mother her dying wish."

Belle closed her eyes, and for a moment, she considered that Bethany might be speaking the truth. Such power could be enough to turn a person mad. And God only knew that Noah had the inclination.

Bethany placed a hand on Belle's shoulder. "Dear Arabella. I had nearly lost all hope after my lawyers failed and then I remembered you. When I met you, I thought it strange at the time that my nephew seemed to have his sights set on someone so, well common,

"My dear, it is a cruel truth, but I'm sure you have realized it yourself. And then it occurred to me. You were a patsy. He intended to use you to conceal the ring from me. That's why he kept you around. Didn't you ever wonder? Oh, my dear child, believe me I know the pain of unrequited love. It makes us do crazy things, doesn't it? And I'm sure he did care for you in some, small way. Some may even call it love. But you've done all you can now, dear. You've played your part. And if you truly love him, won't you do what's best for him? Even if he cannot do it for himself?"

Belle found that she was short of breath as the seeds of doubt that had lain dormant within her burst forth in flower. What if Bethany was right? What if everything Belle had ever feared were true? But then she thought of Noah, of the trust he had placed in her, of the aching love she had felt and still felt, and she knew it didn't matter.

"You're wasting your time," Belle said between clenched teeth as the heat of anger rose within her. "Even if what you are saying is true, it doesn't change anything."

"Then you are a fool," Bethany whispered harshly, her lips tightening as she glared down her nose at Belle. "I didn't track you down and come all this way to the middle of nowhere to be told I've wasted my time."

"Maybe I am a fool," Belle lifted her chin. "But I'm telling you the truth. I don't have the ring. Noah took it back with him when he returned to Sydney. I would imagine that he had it locked away the moment he arrived. You're too late."

Bethany made a vicious sound, like a cat hissing at a rival. "Liar," she spat, her features twisting with rage. "You have it. You must have it. Give it to me."

Belle stood her ground beneath Bethany Faye's withering stare. And as she looked at the older woman's face, pinched with hatred and desperation, she didn't feel intimidated any more. All she felt was pity. "I don't have it," she repeated evenly. "I'm sorry."

Bethany held her gaze for what felt like an eternity. And then, abruptly, she swept up her long, flowing skirt and turned on her heel. In an instant she had cleared the backyard, swung open the fly-screen door and stalked through the house, the battered door clattering noisily in her wake.

Mum came bustling out in to the yard before Belle could catch her breath. "What in the world was that about? What did that woman want?"

"That was Noah's aunt," Belle smiled, feeling oddly calm after her ordeal.

"Well, yes, I gathered that, darl. But why did she come here? And what on earth was she raving on about for so long? The nerve of her, accusing you of lying. Arabella, what is going on?"

"It was a misunderstanding," Belle shrugged and sighed, taking her mother by the arm. "She believed that I was hanging on to something that didn't belong to me. But she was wrong."

# Chapter Thirty-Eight

One week in early October, after six days of solid rain drenched Pitts in floods, the sun came out.

It got downright hot that Saturday afternoon and Mum had been preparing dinner when the phone rang. She hurriedly shook off her oven mitts and ran to the phone, wiping her moist brow with one hand as she grasped the receiver in the other. A second later, she dropped the phone and shrieked Belle's name at the top of her lungs.

"What is it?" Belle panted as she entered the kitchen with her hand over her chest. "What's the matter? Is it bad news?"

But Mum turned around and her eyes were gleaming. "It's far from that," she said, looking stunned. "It's Sidney. He's awake."

\*\*\*

Belle and her mother bolted through the hospital corridors, two minds pulsing with only one thought. They reached Sidney's room and were greeted by a doctor and two nurses who were hovering by the doorway.

"Let me see him," Mum begged, peering frantically over the doctor's shoulder. "Is he okay? Can he talk? Can he hear me? Sidney. Sidney."

The doctor placed her hand on Mum's arm. "He's awake, he's lucid, but he's weak and confused," she explained gently. "I know it's difficult, but try to take a deep breath and stay calm before you go in and see him."

Mum nodded, but Belle could see she was still focused on getting in to the room. She touched her mother's hand. "Mum. Take a deep breath," she repeated, taking one herself. "Sid's been asleep for a long time. He's not going to know what's going on."

The doctor inclined her head in agreement and Mum sighed, running her hands over her face. She took a shaky breath then another and several more until she was breathing more or less normally. Then she nodded. "Okay. All right. I'm calm. Can I see him now?"

The doctor smiled and stepped aside. "He's all yours," she said softly and Belle and her mother looked at each other for a moment. Then Mum took Belle's hand and they crept past the nurses and into the room.

The afternoon sun streamed through the blinds, and onto the white, narrow bed where Sidney was sitting upright, facing the window. When they neared the bed he turned and his tired, pale little face lit up in a smile.

Belle thought her heart would burst and Mu, clutched her chest, uttering a single, guttural sob of relief.

"Sorry," was the first thing Sidney said as his mother and sister approached him, Belle took his hand and Mum stroked his forehead and kissed him over and over. His voice was soft and hoarse from disuse, but to Belle it was the most wonderful sound she had ever heard.

"Sorry?" Mum exclaimed, clapping her hand over her mouth as her voice echoed in the quiet room. Tears streamed down her face as she looked at her son. "Darling, you're the last person in the world who should ever be sorry. I'm sorry. I'm so sorry, Sidney."

"Iss fine fo me," Sid said with a feeble shrug. "I don remember a thing. But when they tol me what happened, I knew you'd be worried."

Mum shook her head, blinking furiously. "My brave, beautiful boy." She pressed a sound kiss to his cheek and gazed at him with wet, adoring eyes.

"Welcome back," Belle whispered, smiling through her tears. She couldn't take her eyes off her brother. He was awake. He was awake exactly as she had dreamed he would be. She squeezed his hand and he looked at her and gave a weak grin.

"Thaks Beyya. Iss good to be back. They tol me I wass out fo five and a half months. I bet you thought I wass never gonna wake up."

Belle and her mum looked at each other but didn't say a word. Belle lifted Sidney's hand and kissed it. "I always knew you'd come back," she whispered. "Do you remember anything? Could you hear us talking to you?"

Sidney furrowed his brow. "I don remember anything. I don even remember how this happened. But I thik I dreamed about you. Both of you. They were nice dreams." He sighed and leaned back against his pillow.

Belle and her mum shared another look.

"Do you feel all right?" Mum asked. "Are you tired? Thirsty? Hungry?"

Sidney smiled. "No. I fine. They tol me they gonna run some tests to check my brain for damage but I don thik they need to. I fine, I thik. I don feel any different. I juss wanna go home."

"And we want you home too, little bro. So much. It hasn't been the same without you. But I think you'll probably need to stay here for a little longer. Just until they're sure everything's okay."

Sidney nodded and closed his eyes and Belle leaned forward and kissed him on the forehead. She gazed lovingly at his smooth, pale skin and bruised eyelids, reaching out to trace her fingers over his soft, brown hair. She turned to Daisy and smiled. She knew they had been given what so few people received in life.

A second chance.

\*\*\*

Belle flopped on her bed, her arms stretched over her head, a wide, happy grin on her lips. She rolled onto her stomach, gazing out at the bright, new sliver of moon and felt a sense of peace she couldn't remember having felt before. As her eyes followed the silver rays of light, they fell upon the Autumn Flame, and right at the tip of the highest branch sat a new, golden bud.

# Chapter Thirty-Nine

Belle woke from a dream and the sun was streaming through her window. It was the last day of school and she had dreamed that she was standing with Sidney in the kitchen, holding an acceptance letter in her hand that entitled her to study fine arts at the University of New South Wales.

Smiling, Belle stumbled from her bed and crossed the room to the vanity dresser. Blinking at her rumpled reflection. Sometime during night, the moist spring air had caused her carefully straightened hair to curl. She sighed and went to flick the switch on her hair straightener when she stopped, her hand hovering over the device. She looked once more at her reflection and for a moment saw the old Belle, the girl she had been before she'd ever set eyes on Noah Cole.

Sure, her hair was a little wild. Her features were plain without makeup to enhance them. But it was who she was. Had she been holding onto Noah, to an illusion, ever since he left? It had been over four months and she still wore the clothes he had given her, straightened her hair the way he liked it, and associated with people she wasn't sure she cared about.

Hadn't she and Noah parted because she had wanted to be herself? So why was she still clinging to a fantasy?

Belle frowned, raked her fingers through her hair, and swept the crimson ringlets in to a ponytail. With one last glance at her reflection, she smiled and threw on an old pair of jeans and a t-shirt. Then she left for her final day of high school.

There was a buzz of excitement in the air from the moment Belle stepped foot on school grounds. People were dressed in casual clothes, balloons and streamers were hung everywhere and everyone she passed was smiling. It wasn't a dream. It really was the last day of high school. Exams were over. There were no more assignments. Classes were finished for good.

Belle could hardly believe it.

Ben Carter did a double take when he saw her in her casual clothes with her curls pulled loosely back. He raised his brows and Belle smiled boldly, inviting any comment he might throw her way. Go on, she thought. Give it your best shot. After all, wasn't it fitting that her school life should end the way it had began?

But Ben returned her smile and sauntered up to greet her. "Hey babe. Gone casual, huh? Good call. All the girls have really gone overboard, I reckon. Check out Brianna," he sniggered as Brianna stood on tiptoe to reach one of the balloons that had been tied to a post. She was holding a pin and she used it to puncture the balloon with a loud *pop*. She laughed hysterically as did several people standing nearby, possibly because her dress was so short that they all caught a glimpse of her undies.

Belle couldn't help but giggle as she slid Ben a curious glance. What was his deal? Had he actually grown a brain over the past few months?

"Have you thought about going to the formal?" Ben asked, trying to sound nonchalant. "I know it's not your thing, but everyone else is paired up, ya know. Makes sense for us to go together."

Belle bit her lip to stop herself from smiling. "I haven't decided whether I'm going or not," she said truthfully. "I'll think about it, Carter."

Ben straightened his shoulders and ran a hand over his short, curly hair. He nodded. "Right. Cool. No worries. Well, let me know what you decide, hey?"

Belle smiled. "I will."

In the distance, a tall thin boy and a petite girl in a pretty blue dress were watching their exchange. When Belle realized it was Susie and John she smiled and waved, the buzz in the air and her newfound confidence making her bold.

Susie hesitated then gave a half smile and lifted her hand slightly. Belle took it as a good sign. As she approached them she saw Susie shoot John a meaningful look. He inclined his head then quirked a quick smile in Belle's direction and made himself scarce.

"Hey," Belle said, feeling suddenly awkward. She stopped a couple of meters from where Susie sat and shoved her hands in her pockets.

"Hey," Susie said primly, folding her hands in her lap.

"Uh, so, are you excited about the end of school?"

Susie raised an eyebrow. "Isn't everyone?"

Belle sighed. Susie wasn't going to make it easy for her to make amends. She decided to skip the formalities. "Look, Susie. I'm sorry, okay? I know things have been different between us. I haven't been around much. I should have, I don't know. I should have spent more time with you. Or tried to include you in stuff, I guess."

Susie eyed Belle suspiciously. "Yeah. You should have."

"I know you wanted to hang out with Brianna and all of those guys. I could have invited you, but I thought you were angry that... I don't know. That I was hanging out with them when that's what you always wanted."

Susie's expression changed. She eyed Belle with something close to pity in her eyes. "You know what? That's where you're wrong. Yeah, I was jealous at first, but then when I saw the way you changed, that you'd do anything Noah said, and always hung around with those morons. And that you thought you were hot stuff in all your little designer outfits and all that, I guess I figured out I didn't really want that after all. I mean, it's so fake. And stupid." She sighed, adjusting her glasses. "But I guess, I could have been more supportive or something. I could have actually talked to you about it."

Belle gave a small smile. "Yeah. I could have talked to you about it too. And you're right. It is fake. And stupid. And believe me, I know that. It was interesting though. I guess, even after everything, I'm kind of glad it all happened. Even if it was crazy. There's so much I want to tell you."

Susie bit her lip as she looked at Belle. She sighed. And then she inhaled suddenly and clasped her hands under her chin. "Oh Belle. I have so much to tell you. I can't even believe how long it's been. I put my preferences in to do medicine, and if I aced my exams like I think I did, I might actually get in. And there's so much more. I wanted to tell you about John and everything." She paused and cringed, shooting Belle a sympathetic look. "Sorry. About Noah, now that he's gone and everything. Are you all right?"

Belle considered the question. She hadn't been fine, not for a long time. She remembered the dark nights when she'd thought of nothing but finding a way to escape the pain. But by then, things were different. And though the ache in her heart had not entirely disappeared, it had eased with time. And she supposed that some day it would be gone.

"Yeah," Belle said with a lift of her chin. "Yeah. I'm okay."

Susie looked relieved and they were quiet for a moment. Then her lips tweaked in a little smirk. "You know, I'm not going to say it, Quinn."

Belle rolled her eyes. "Yeah, I know. You told me so."

Susie smiled sheepishly then grabbed Belle's arm on an impulse, a spark lighting her eyes as she looked up at her. "But you have to tell me something."

Belle looked down at Susie in surprise. "Sure. What?"

"Was he a good kisser?"

Belle blinked for a moment. Then she burst out laughing. She kept laughing for so long her sides ached and tears sprung to her eyes. She wiped them away to see Susie sitting with her arms folded, looking at her expectantly.

"Well?"

Belle giggled once more, then composed herself. She looked at her friend and sighed wistfully, pulling a strand of hair back from her cheek. "Yeah. He was a good kisser. He was good at a lot of things."

Susie's eyes widened and Belle gave a nod and a secretive smile. Then Susie squealed and they both dissolved in to giggles.

# Chapter Forty

On the same day as Sidney took two unassisted steps from his wheelchair to the kitchen table, a letter addressed to Arabella Quinn arrived in the mail. Thinking it was too soon for university acceptance letters, Mum snatched it up and eyed it curiously. She dropped it in front of Belle as she sat eating her breakfast.

"What's this?" Belle asked between mouthfuls of cereal.

Mum shrugged. "Not sure, love. But it's got a funny looking logo on it. Something about an exhibition."

Belle nearly choked on her cornflakes. She swallowed the lump of flakes, and grabbed the letter, tearing it open and unfolding the piece of paper with trembling fingers.

"Mum," she whispered after she had skimmed the page, her face turning white. "I got in."

"What?" Mum peered over Belle's shoulder. "To uni? Already?"

"No," Belle turned her gaze on her mother. "My drawing. It got into the annual art competition."

Mum furrowed her brow. "Art competition?" she queried. Then her eyes lit up as she understood. "Baby Belle, that's wonderful. Congratulations, darling, I'm so proud of you."

Belle nodded but she was still in shock. She barely registered it as her mother wrapped her in a bear hug and pressed a wet kiss to her cheek. Only Sidney's jubilant guffaw awoke her from her trance. "I knew it," he laughed. "My sister tha artist. Don forget me when yo famous, okay?"

Belle's face broke out in a smile and she squeezed her mother tightly. Then she knelt down and wrapped her arms around her brother. "As if, Sid," she said, beaming up at him. "Never in a million years."

\*\*\*

There it was, her portrait displayed for the world to see. It hung on the wall of Pitts Art Gallery, framed in a sleek, black border with her full name and a brief description printed beneath it. And beside the frame was a bright blue ribbon with the bold inscription: *First Prize.*

Belle's hands were still shaking from the whirlwind of emotion, from the surprise announcement, the influx of congratulations, and the blinding shutter of camera flashes. Mum had wept with pride and Susie had spent several minutes squealing over the prospect of Belle's photo being in the paper. High-fives and bear hugs had been dealt out, the giant novelty check had been wedged in to the back of Sidney's wheelchair and everyone was standing, holding celebratory glasses of champagne, in front of the reason for all of the commotion.

"Isn't this exciting?" Mum said proudly as she wheeled Sidney closer to where Belle's portrait of Noah hung in the far right corner of the gallery. "Look at it up there. Like a real work of art."

"Iss awesome Beyya," Sidney said, turning to grin over his shoulder at Belle. "Iss tha best one yo ever done."

Belle ducked her head, glowing with pride. "Thanks Sid."

Mum sipped at her champagne and ran her finger along the edge of the giant check. She giggled. "Ten thousand dollars. I still can't believe it. This is going to change everything, Bels. It's going to make all the difference in the world."

Belle nodded, sliding an arm around her mother's waist. She closed her eyes, feeling as close to euphoric as she ever had. "I'm glad I can finally give back some of all you've given me."

"Oh, Bels. What would I do without you?" Mum tilted her head, sighing as she gazed at the picture. "He was handsome, wasn't he?" she murmured, reaching out to squeeze her daughter's hand.

Belle squeezed back and bent down to rest her head on Mum's shoulder. "Yeah," she agreed softly. "He was."

They stared for a moment longer until Mum cleared her throat and announced that she was going to get some refreshments. "Anyone want anything?" she asked.

Belle and Susie shook their heads and Mum shrugged and wheeled Sidney into the next room where they were serving snacks and drinks.

"Do you still miss him?" Susie asked after they'd been standing in silence for a minute or so.

Belle thought for a moment, wondering how much of her private pain to divulge. She had kept it inside for so long but she considered that perhaps it might be time to unburden herself. "Yes," she admitted. "Every day."

Susie made a sympathetic noise and squeezed her friend's shoulder. "It sucks, Belle. It really does. But you know what? He wasn't worthy of you. I mean, look at you now. You're going to be a famous artist some day and he'll be some guy you hooked up with in high school."

Belle smiled, grateful for Susie's support. But she knew in her heart that it wasn't true. Noah was worthy of being loved. And she was glad she had loved him. Even if her love had not been returned in the way she'd hoped, she could never regret having felt it. Noah had turned her ordinary little life on its end, had challenged her to look within and beyond herself. And for that, she would always be grateful.

"Speak of the devil," she heard Susie whisper urgently. "Belle, I don't want to freak you out, but... "

Belle turned her head and when she followed Susie's gaze she knew exactly what the matter was. A shiver ran down her spine. There, in the doorway, a familiar figure stood unmoving, watching her with an impenetrable expression. Susie coughed, muttered something, and made herself scarce and suddenly it seemed that the people had all melted away, and it was only the two of them, standing beneath the portrait of a troubled young man. He approached her and when he reached her side she struggled to think of something to say. And when, at last, she thought of something her voice caught in her throat.

"What did you say, red?"

Belle's heartbeat skipped at the sound of her nickname. His voice was as she remembered it. She swallowed, finding that her mouth was quite dry. "I said, hello."

Noah smiled slowly, his eyes twinkling. "Hello," he replied. His smile broadened when he noticed her hair. "You look well."

Belle could only gaze at him as she nodded. He was real. He was there. He looked the same with his mane of hair and iridescent eyes. But he seemed warmer, older somehow.

"I heard about Sidney," he said softly, looking at her. "I'm happy for you. For your family."

A smile touched Belle's lips. "Thank you," she said, meaning it. "How did know?"

"I check in with the guys occasionally." Noah shrugged. "The last time I spoke to them, they told me he'd been discharged." He looked down, raking a hand through his hair. "I wasn't checking on you. But I wanted to make sure."

"Oh." Belle felt a pang of hurt that he had kept in touch with everyone but her. And that no one had even bothered to tell her. But when she realized what he had done, she felt something else entirely.

"I thought you might like to know that dear Aunt Bethany will be receiving a lovely candle holder and my mother's collection of stamps from the estate. And nothing more."

"Oh." Belle's eyes widened and then she smiled. She wondered if she should tell him about his aunt's impromptu visit but decided that, for the time being, she would keep it to herself. "That's great news."

"It is," Noah agreed. "My faith in karma is renewed."

They smiled at each other until Belle's heart began to flutter and she was forced to lower her eyes. She couldn't believe he was really there. Standing before her, speaking to her, when she thought she would never see him again.

When she looked up, Noah was staring at her. She caught her breath as he reached out to tuck a strand of hair behind her ear, and then she feared she might start to cry.

"Ah, red," Noah sighed and she wondered if he noticed that she was trembling. "You were true to your word, weren't you?" He gestured to the portrait of himself that hung on the wall beside them. "You did what you set out to do. I'm impressed. But you were wrong about one thing. You're not going to wind up a failed artist. Quite the opposite, in fact." He smiled and Belle took in the fact that he had paid her an extraordinary compliment.

"You're not mad, then?" she asked, glancing at the sketch. "I didn't think you'd be here. So I I thought you wouldn't see it."

"Don't worry." Noah shook his head. "I'm not as proud as I once was. So no, Belle, I'm not mad. I'm grateful."

Belle looked at Noah curiously, but he straightened himself and glanced toward the doorway. "I can't stay long. I only came to say congratulations. You should be proud of yourself." He leaned down and kissed her cheek and Belle's eyes fluttered closed.

It was as though no time had passed, he still affected her so strongly. She felt the lance of separation as he pulled away. They stared at each other and Belle clenched her hands to stop herself reaching for him.

"I'll see you at the formal, then," he said as he moved to leave.

Belle's eyes widened. "Excuse me?"

Noah smiled and Belle found herself mesmerized. "Well, I've been invited. And you don't think I'd turn down an evening at the glamorous Pitts High School hall, do you?" he grinned and raised his brows.

Belle felt quite stupid as she stood with her mouth open but Noah gave her no time to respond. "I'll see you soon, then," he said, touching a hand to her shoulder. "Goodbye, Belle."

And as he began to walk away, Belle noticed something that caused her heart to pause in its fluttering. Something that glinted in the bright gallery lights, something gold and solid on the pinkie finger of Noah's left hand.

His father's ring.

# Chapter Forty-One

Belle, Susie and John piled in to John's car, giggling and breathless with excitement. They laughed and sang and made jokes, filled with vigor and the buzz of their first half-glass of champagne. John looked quite dashing in a pin striped suit, Susie wore a black halter dress and a tiara in her hair, and Belle was sporting a flowing, strapless, pale blue dress that came to her knees, with her hair coiled back in a French twist, courtesy of Susie's amateur hairdressing skills. The girls had applied make-up to one another, and though neither of them was particularly accomplished at the art, they both managed to look quite prettily made up.

The hall was decorated with balloons, colored lights and streamers, and was already full of people by the time they arrived. There was a live band on stage, and Susie squealed when they started playing one of her favorite songs. She grabbed Belle's arm with one hand and John's with the other and led them on to the dance floor where a few couples had already begun to dance. They giggled as they tried to move together in a threesome, but eventually John and Susie drew closer to each other and Belle was left on the outskirts, hovering awkwardly as all the couples moved and swayed. She was about to escape to the refreshment table when Ben and Anastasia approached her.

"Belle. You decided to show." Ben grinned, looking rather respectable in a simple, plain black suit and tie combination. Anastasia was stunning in a clingy red dress that accentuated her figure and highlighted the glossy color of her hair. "You've got balls, coming by yourself."

Bell ducked her head. "Well, I'm not exactly…" but then she trailed off. She'd never actually agreed to meet Noah, that maybe he hadn't been serious about it in the first place. Had she been insanely stupid going to the formal based on the slim chance of him showing up?

"Don't worry, Belle," Anastasia said smugly. "There are plenty of leftovers waiting for a dance if you get desperate." She giggled as she gestured to a line of single boys who were standing against the wall, looking tense and uncomfortable as they watched all the others dancing and drinking and enjoying themselves. Belle felt a tug of sympathy for them before she realized she was no different.

"Or you could borrow me for a bit," Ben suggested but Anastasia jabbed him in the ribs and he winced. "Ow. Fine, forget it. Sorry Quinn."

Belle gave a half smile. "S'okay. I'm not really that into dancing anyway. You guys have fun."

"We will," Anastasia smiled sweetly as she led Ben out on to the dance floor. Belle watched them go, remembering that once, not so long ago, neither of the two would have acknowledged her presence unless it was to hurl an insult or use her for target practice. At first, the year had seemed like any other, but so soon it had raced by and as it was drawing to a close, it seemed that nothing was quite as it had been before.

Belle felt older, wiser, and she knew that an irreplaceable piece of her innocence had been lost forever.

She sighed, deciding that she needed some fresh air. As she turned to approach the exit she saw that someone was blocking it and when she focused her heart stood still. Noah looked impossibly debonair in a tailored suit with a twinkle in his eye and a grin that revealed his perfect, white teeth.

"Looking good, red," he said in a low voice, stepping toward her. "I wasn't sure you'd come."

Belle's cheeks grew warm. "You weren't?"

Noah smiled and shrugged. "I had my doubts." He held out his arm and she took it, following him through the door and out in to the warm, spring air.

"I wasn't sure you'd show, either," she admitted.

Noah chuckled. "I knew you'd say that," he replied. "Oh ye of little faith."

The huge maple tree that shaded a portion of the playground was decorated with fairy lights and Belle looked up at them, enjoying the soft glow they cast over the leaves and branches. There was something magical about fairy lights. They made the familiar, old playground where she had spent so many lunchtimes seem a different place entirely.

They sat on the seat where they had sketched together all those months ago and Noah picked up a maple leaf and began twirling it between his fingers. He glanced at Belle and smiled.

"You look different," he stated.

Belle grimaced. "Yeah. I know." She gestured to her curled hair and second-hand dress. "The hair. The clothes."

But Noah chuckled. "No. It's not that. There's something else. Something more."

Belle stared at her lap, not knowing what to say.

"You look lovely," he said in a low voice, discarding the leaf and placing a hand over hers.

Belle's pulse quickened and she wondered if he could feel it. "Oh really? Even though this dress is from the Op Shop?"

Noah grinned. "Yup."

"Even though my hair's all wild and woolly? Even though I'm not pretty anymore?"

Noah released a slow breath. "You've always been beautiful, Belle," he murmured, and there was a sadness to his tone that surprised her. Lost for words, she stared at his hand in her lap. "Have you missed me?" he whispered as his fingers tightened around hers. The note of uncertainty in his voice made her heart ache.

"Yes," she replied.

He sighed as though her confession relieved him. He brought her hand to his lips and kissed it gently. "I never really noticed this tree before," he commented after a beat, looking up at the golden-leafed branches. "It's pretty. I can't believe it's been here all along. It's amazing what you can overlook, what can be right in front of you all along, only you're too blind to see it."

Belle looked at him and frowned. It was then she remembered the ring he was wearing at the art gallery that day. She glanced at his left hand and sure enough there it was, the golden collet glinting beneath the twinkling lights.

"I've got something to tell you, Belle." Noah sighed, caressing her fingers. She shivered at his touch, at the serious tone of his voice.

"What is it?" she whispered. She reached over to trace the ring, lifting her eyes to Noah's in question.

He returned her gaze, his eyes burning in to hers. Then he exhaled and looked down. He reached in to his pocket and withdrew something that looked to be a photograph and handed it to Belle without a word.

Belle peered at the photo. In it, a young girl of about seven or eight years of age was sitting at a table with a plate before her. A mop of strawberry blonde hair framed her elfin, fine-boned face, and a pair of bright blue eyes gazed out from beneath a thicket of tawny lashes. She was tiny, frail looking, yet beautiful. And covered quite thoroughly from the chin down in what appeared to be chocolate cake.

Belle sucked in a rapid breath. "Is this...?"

"Yes." Noah's eyes seemed to mist over for a moment as he glanced at the photo and then back at Belle. "That's her. That's Lucy."

Belle felt her jaw drop and her heart begin to throb. "You met her?"

"I did." Belle stared at the photo, dumbfounded, and when Noah saw her expression, he chuckled. "You're surprised."

"I... well, yes." Belle confessed, gazing at Noah. "I mean, I thought... Noah. This is huge. I can't believe it."

"What can I say? I guess I have a heart, after all," Noah murmured with a twist of his lips.

Belle was struck by the sudden urge to throw her arms around his neck. "Of course you do," she whispered, beaming. "You always have."

Noah smiled ruefully, shaking his head. "I know what my mother said. I know what she'd told me, what she wanted. But after I returned to the empty house, after I was left there with everything, *everything* I had wanted, it felt hollow. And it made me think. I started to question things. I started wanting answers. What use is it having everything when you have no one to share it with?" He glanced at the photograph that Belle still held between her fingers and the corner of his mouth twitched. "I figured that if I was going to live by my mother's laws, I may as well take it upon myself to find out the truth behind them. I'd been clinging to her memory, holding on to something that..." his eyes darkened and he trailed off, his hands clenching.

"Noah?" Belle reached out and placed her hand over his. "Are you okay?"

Noah nodded, composing himself. "My mother was wrong, Belle. He loved her. Alice, I mean. My father loved her. I read his letters."

"Letters?"

Noah looked at her, a strange, new light in his eyes. "Yes. When I went to visit Alice and Lucy..." his voice caught and he paused for a moment. "Alice looked so different, Belle. I mean, she still has that crazy hair. She's still lovely. But she seemed so tired. And she had this terrible cough that sounded like she was hacking up a lung. You should have seen the place. No one should have to live like that," his eyes darkened and his hands clenched once more. "And Lucy. Look at her, Belle. I can see my father in her. I can see myself."

Belle nodded, tears springing to her eyes. She clasped Noah's hand and he squeezed back, bringing her hand to his lips and kissing it soundly. "Alice embraced me as though I were her own son. I can't describe how that felt. It's as though...I don't know.

"It's like a part of me, a memory or something I'd never let myself feel all came rushing back. We talked for hours. And then she showed me the letters my father wrote to her. They describe everything. The falsehood of my parents' marriage, my father's feelings for Alice, their affair, his suspicions about my mother."

Belle raised her eyebrows and Noah nodded. "I found out everything. *Everything*, Belle. I feel like I didn't understand anything until now. It's if as though I've been looking at everything through frosted glass. And now, I can see. It's like a spell had been put on me and now I guess it's broken." He gave a hollow laugh. "That sounds so pathetic."

Belle stared at him, trying to make sense of the fragments of the story. "It's not pathetic," she whispered, tracing his face with her fingertips. She leaned in to kiss his cheek and Noah turned swiftly, cupped her face in his hands and kissed her.

Belle responded at once, her hands clutching his shoulders to draw him closer but he pulled away as abruptly, gazing in to her eyes for a moment before releasing a shaky breath. "I should have listened to my heart, Belle. I've wasted so much time. Hating my father, blaming Alice. But it was never her fault, or his. They were pawns in a game. It was a game that led to all of this. It was my mother all along, Belle."

Belle gasped and Noah looked at her with haunted eyes. "She orchestrated the whole thing. She quite literally drove him to it. She never loved him. Not really. She only ever wanted the prestige, the money, the social standing. That's why she married him." He was staring into Belle's eyes as though he was begging her to understand. She stroked his hand, urging him on.

"My father knew, Belle. He figured it out in the end, but by then it was too late. She was the one who hired Alice in the first place, she was the one who planted the seeds in everyone's thoughts, she was the one who convinced him to change his will and who leaked the scandal to the press so that when it all went down she would be left with everything. And he knew that my mother would never let him live it down, that she would take him for everything he had. God, it's so clear now. How could I have been so Goddamn blind, so stupid? All these years it was her fault. Her fault."

Noah bowed his head and made an anguished sound and Belle pulled him against her, her heart wrenching as she felt a single, hot tear splash against her throat. She soothed her hands over his back, grappling to understand it all. It had all been a game. His mother had planned it from the beginning. And she had used all of them, mercilessly, even Noah, her own flesh and blood. Her son. Belle could only imagine Noah's agony.

And for one shameful moment she felt glad that his mother was dead.

"You were a child," she told him, running her fingers through his hair. "How could you have known? People make mistakes. They can be deceived and led astray. They don't always do what's right. But you can, Noah. You have. You were so brave to do what you did." She looked at the photograph that had slipped from her fingers and in to her lap and released a deep, shuddery breath. "What you've done is amazing."

"Thank you," Noah choked out. "For everything." He gripped Belle's hand, keeping his head low as his chest heaved with each unsteady breath.

Eventually, he raised his eyes and Belle saw that they were gleaming. "I am going to fix this," he said clearly. "If it's the last thing I do, I'm going to put things right. With Alice and Lucy and the inheritance. With you."

Belle felt as though her heart would burst with the sudden rush of love that filled it. She lifted her hand to touch Noah's cheek and he closed his eyes.

"He was a good man. Despite everything, I swear. He was a good man. He was weak, and he let her win. He didn't have the strength to fight her anymore. And while I never will truly understand why he did what he did, I know that he thought he didn't have a choice." He turned his cheek against Belle's palm with a sigh. His eyes were bright and full of sorrow.

"I believe in you," Belle whispered. Noah's shoulders lifted and his lip twitched in a half smile. "And in his letters he's left you an amazing gift. I think maybe he knew that there is a strength in you that he never had. And now you've been given the gift of understanding. You can put things right. And you know what? You're not alone anymore. You have a sister. You have family. I'm so proud of you, Noah. I don't know what else to say."

Noah turned his gaze on Belle's face. And after a moment, he smiled. It was a slow, tender smile that transformed him, lighting his eyes. "Arabella Quinn," he whispered her name like a prayer, "how are you so good? I've treated you terribly. I can see that now. You will never know how sorry I am. I've spent months building up the courage to tell you, to ask for your forgiveness even though I know I don't deserve it. I was wrong, about so many things. But now I can see for the first time in my life. And I see you.

"Can you forgive me? Can you find it in you to love an untamed heart?" He nuzzled her palm then turned and kissed it gently. "Because I love you. With all my heart I love you. My sweet, beautiful Belle."

"I'm afraid it's too late," Belle whispered, and Noah jerked back. As joy filled her soul she put him out of his misery. "I already love you. I always have." Noah's face lit up and laughter rose in Belle's chest and bubbled out of her mouth. "But promise me something?"

Noah took both of Belle's hands in his. "Anything."

"Promise that from now on, you'll be yourself. No games, no pretenses. Just you. And me. Like this. We're perfect exactly the way we are, Noah."

And before he could protest, she threw her arms around his neck and pressed her lips to his. With a stifled moan, Noah clutched her against him and returned the kiss until they were both breathless. And when they parted, he was smiling.

"You do realize something though, red, don't you?" he said, fingering a stray wisp of her hair and pushing it back from her face.

"Oh?" Belle murmured, pressing kisses to Noah's cheek.

"We're going to have to do something about this hair."

Belle went rigid and pulled back to regard Noah with a look of horror. And when she saw that his eyes were wet and he was shaking with laughter, she pulled in a sharp breath and did something she'd wanted to do from the moment she set eyes on him. She slapped him. Soundly.

Noah froze and for several long moments Belle could only stare at him, her mouth agape. An apology felt ready to burst forth when Noah pressed a finger to her lips, smiled, and leaned in to whisper in her ear.

"Yes," he said softly. "I deserved that."

# ABOUT THE AUTHOR

Alexandra Wright has been writing since she could put pen to paper. Growing up in Sydney, Australia, she took pleasure in playing the piano, singing, the arts, languages, cooking, and of course she spent a great deal of time reading and writing. Having so many interests meant her career aspirations had a habit of changing, but her profession eventually chose her. An incurable obsession with literature, her earliest and most enduring passion, led her to a career as a novelist. She dabbled in writing short stories and novellas as a child and teen, and began writing full-length novels as an adult. Still a child at heart, and an educator of young children, it was a natural progression for her to move into writing fiction for children and young adults.

# ALSO BY ALEXANDRA WRIGHT

*Collision*
*Empath*

www.BOROUGHSPUBLISHINGGROUP.com

If you enjoyed this book, please write a review. Our authors appreciate the feedback, and it helps future readers find books they love. We welcome your comments and invite you to send them to info@boroughspublishinggroup.com. Follow us on Facebook, Twitter and Instagram, and be sure to sign up for our newsletter for surprises and new releases from your favorite authors.

Are you an aspiring writer? Check out www.boroughspublishinggroup.com/submit and see if we can help you make your dreams come true.